The Twin Cities
Cifiscape Vol. I

I0533686

Written by
Ken Avidor • Brian Garrity • Max
Hrabal • Bob Lipski • Ken Lubold
•Aaron Wilson • Toianna Gump

Edited by
Kit Martin • Jeffrey Martin • Zach West
Mika Thuening •Hannah Byrnes-Enoch

Published by Onyx Neon Press, United States

ISBN 0-9779201-4-3   ISBN-13 978-0-9779201-4-3

First Edition 2010

Cover Art by Ken Avidor

Designed and Typeset by Jeffrey Martin

www.onyxneon.com

Index

The Twin Cities
Cifiscape Vol. I

INTRODUCTION

"All things fall and are built again,
And those that build them again are gay."
– William Yeats
"Lapis Lazuli"

We are proud to present Cifiscape vol. I, The Twin Cities: a collection of what the metro could become from seven authors' perspectives. Cifiscape asks the reader to think of our future. The question strives to shape our expectations: sharing our dreams and nightmares, it narrates the best and worst. We are a group of editors, writers and illustrators who have come together under Onyx Neon Press. Through Cifiscape vol. I, we want to share stories of the Twin Cities, written by the Twin Cities.

With this mission in mind, the authors were asked to narrate a short story based in, around, or under the Metro of the future. The authors were picked for their relevance to the theme and the clarity of their writing. Here we are excited to have worked with authors presenting seven possible moments in our future.

For The Killing of The Happiest Man

Max Hrabal brings us into the celebration of the Happiest Man. The Regional commission declares a regional celebration, 'Happiest Man Day', to boost moral. One man cannot take this shit.

The Prisoner

Ken Lubold delves into the mind of a 21st century executive. Driven to succeed, he pays the ultimate price.

Bicyclopolis

Ken Avidor draws us into a startling vision of the future: bicycle-knights rule the metro, and clouds of bags choke out civilization. One man's lost journal brings collapse to the fore.

Godless

Brian Garrity blazes through a street fight in front of the Triple Rock. Employing rough style, and life like dialogue, the warriors of the future beat a heady rhythm while taking on the dominate upper class.

What's For Dinner

Aaron Wilson depicts a future where supply of fresh food has become a religious experience. Live well and poor, or live fat and cheap.

Ill Communication
Bob Lipinski's Uptown Girl gets an assignment: what will the Twin Cities be like in 100 years?

Thinker's Lure
Toianna Gump gives us a home coming. After years away, Guy returns to his family. Despite his fear of the Community, he tries to save his son.

In the stories I am struck by the idea of hope. I noticed that the submissions were dystopic: collapsing society, oppressive technology, oppressive expectations. This pessimism seems to derive from the theme of Cifiscape: what will the Twin Cities be in the future. 'Life is messy,' seems to be the unanimous response of the authors. Thus, setting a story in an actual place - with all of its complexity - requires failings in order to be believable. Unlike Thomas Moore's Utopian no place, Onyx Neon asked authors to project into their actual reality. On the one hand, ideal reality is fine in some far flung universe. On the other hand, in our own town, dangerous possibilities manifest with more dreadful consequences. As a result, I think the submissions painted a gritty picture of the future. The roughness of the edges in the narrations struck me. Structures collapse and institutions incipient under side become apparent. Reading through, this accidental theme, made me wonder why unrelated authors share so much in common.

I realized that for the future to be seen as worse than the present, decline must be the most obvious result. In order for decline to be more likely than development, order must be prevalent in our everyday lives. In other words, we must think the current world is pretty good because improvements do not present themselves readily. For example, I thought about what kind of submissions a Cifiscape Baghdad might receive. In fifty or a hundred years, The Green Zone will probably be gone, families will work, government will provide services, life will be on track. In short, I think Iraqi writers would be more optimistic about the future, because they are dreaming in chaos today.

A hopeful outlook on the future, suggests individuals see obvious solutions to today's problems. Ironically, reticence when imagining the future suggests the world we live in today is not obviously broken. Though there are problems, their resolution is beyond our imagination. I hope, that by imagining our future together, we can see points of improvement for today. In this light, tales of collapse provide warnings. All things will collapse, but all things will be born. It is when too many necessities of life collapse simultaneously that we have to hope for a better future. We look to Cifiscape for warnings, not because of impending collapse, but because of the immense possibilities future births hold.

So, in the future of the Twin Cities we find unlimited possibilities. The question is, what possibilities do we want to live with each other?

I am proud to present
The Twin Cities, Cifiscape Volume I
Kit Martin

FOR THE KILLING OF THE HAPPIEST MAN
BY MAX HRABAL

On the morning of the first annual International Day of Happiness, Piper Hines descended the seven flights from his apartment to the small café on his building's ground floor. He ordered the usual fried egg in a donut and a medium coffee, and then sat at his usual stool to watch the headlines flash silently on the television screen.

Most of the news was about the new holiday. A recent study had sparked renewed energy in the recent public debate over happiness. It found that over fifty percent of the world's population was at least eighty percent likely to be diagnosable as clinically depressed. To do their part at the local level, the Regional Council decided that a set of initiatives and a holiday were in order.

On screen, a bald headed man with thick glasses walked among screaming, ecstatic crowds. It was Garret J. Peterson, the much lauded "Happiest Man in Hennepin County" and Grand Marshal of the first ever Happiness Parade. Garret J. Peterson was a figurehead of growing importance in what was coming to be called the Happiness Movement. He chaired the unofficial Happiness political party, and often appeared as a keynote speaker at the rallies and events leading to the declaration of the holiday.

To Piper, the International Day of Happiness, international in name only, meant that he got off work early to go to the parades and barbeques, and little else. He had a hard time believing that a holiday would make people happy, let alone any of the other recent Happiness Initiatives. He would not even go so far as to admit he was "happy" to be getting off work early. Finishing his coffee while Garret J. Peterson smiled and waved from the reel of recent rallies, Piper just told himself: "I'll take it." and left it at that.

On his way to work, Piper walked over the waterfall in the center of the city. It once flowed freely but now, encased with concrete and enclosed in fiberglass, it was more a guided spill than a fall, with some turbines to make use of gravity's effect on the water. There were plaques on the old bridge with pictures of the way the falls used to look, and a few paragraphs described how the location had evolved to become a great power source for the region. The electricity was transmitted all over the cities, but its first stop was the adjacent engineered garden hanging on the east river bank.

The extensive garden, operated on a city contract by Piper's employer, the Tian Ecosystems Corporation, wrapped around and through the gutted ruins of former grain mills, with a rampart built to match the old stone bridge beside it. It was an architectural marvel, sprawling and coiling in deliberate contrast to the erect, geometric towers of downtown. Standing on the bridge, Piper looked back at the downtown skyline as the dawn struck it. He wilted at its beauty, at what it represented, certainly, but especially at the way the sun sprayed over the glass like paint. It reminded him painfully that he would not see the sun's light for most of the day.

Piper Hines was a sewage technician. He began each day by descending deep underground to the sub sub-basement of the Garden and donning a methane suit. Then he would climb into a Tian Ecosystems "Splasher", a craft designed to move over the surface of the underground lake of sewage, mashing up the larger coagulations, and spraying the smooth derivative to one side. In this manner, the craft worked along the entire batch, making it possible for a "Skimmer" to scoop up the emulsified waste and pump it into the Garden's main fertilizer mixing line. It was a long day ahead of him despite the holiday.

Piper turned away from the dawn and entered past the two main greenhouses, colossal structures of glass and steel. The garden system was partially enclosed, multi-leveled, and terraced, with bridges and walkways connecting a complex of greenhouses and palisades.

In the greenhouses, all manner of plants were grown, with delicately maintained habitats isolated in sealed biomes. Computers handled the moisture distribution and temperature regulation, by way of heaters, sprayers, and artificial sun lights when necessary to stimulate growth. In the winter, citrus trees flourished while snowflakes melted harmlessly on the warm glass domes above. Year round, tomatoes, carrots and corn could be harvested. Moisture drained into a marsh where fish, bug and bacteria colonies worked upon the fallen leaves and other biodetritus. The leavings of the fish and other broken down organic matter then traveled into a chamber below the mushroom caves where they supplemented the human sewage to be worked eventually back in to the garden's fertilization system.

It was not so smelly a job as most people thought when he told them where he worked. There was the sterile methane suit, which provided adequate oxygen, regulated his temperature, kept out the smell, and even played him music when the intercom was not in use. But despite his hygienic interaction with the sewage, and despite the population's consensus that his work was both necessary and good, the fact that he dealt all day with the hidden fluids and excretions of the people aboveground affected the impression he gave and probably, he often suspected, the way he saw others.

Riding the elevator down through the rock and caverns, he remembered seeing a crowd of brightly dressed women and men the previous night, out to the theater or a dining venue downtown. "There goes a bunch of shitters." He had said to himself, the imagined scent in his nostrils. It was no good, he thought, he shouldn't let it get to him. He was doing important work and even if no one appreciated it, he knew it was important. He knew if they stopped to think about it, they would see how valuable he was. It just took more than short-term thought. He could forgive their dismissing him in the short term because he was part of something larger than the short term. What was it the speaker had said at symposium last week? 'Never sacrifice the long term for the sake of the short... nor the short term for the sake of the long.' Or was it that 'the short term loses its value when the long term is neglected?' He couldn't remember. He would have to replay that part of the stream after work.

In the locker room Piper dressed in a cleaned methane suit, then checked out the key to one of the Splashers and began his monotonous shift, methodically ranging over the thick, pasty reservoir, acre by acre turning the waste conglomerate into a more moveable liquid form as an ever constant flow oozed out of the pipes set in the limestone of the cavern's walls.

Over the course of a long shift, to the rhythmic thud of the paddle treads striking into the muck, and whatever music was selected by the management DJs that day, Piper's mind wandered. Every time he settled down in the enclosed cab he was usually still thinking about disliking his job. But eventually this topic wore out and he began to reminisce about his old life, working in the upper levels as a gardener before he was reassigned.

He had loved the openness, the smell of growth and fresh water, and the feel of sunlight on his bare arms. It was different then. He might spend a whole afternoon just plucking raspberries, gently squeezing them away from the branch like jewels handed over reluctantly. Up there he could look at the sky and check the sun's progress. Where is the sun now? He thought, squinting up through his windshield into the glaring floodlights on the cavern ceiling. His memory of those times was limited, and he inevitably moved on.

He thought about the future, and tried to work out all the puzzles of life that confronted him. He often mused that one day he would build his own garden, one where all the produce would be his, and if he had a family by then, it would be for them too. He knew how to do everything. It would not have to be as big as the Tian Ecosystems garden, just enough space to support him at first, and his wife, whoever she might be, and eventually their children, they would grow up and expand the garden and maybe raise their own families there. Piper began to think about how the job he had was not so bad after all. It was easy enough that he could spend hours thinking, at least. Even the sewage job had taught him a thing or two about recycling human waste for use as fertilizer. That was more than most people could say about their work. And he would likely be reassigned again in a few years. There was always something better to look forward to, even if it wasn't going to improve today.

But after a while he put away dreams of having his own garden, looked out over the murky lake of waste and got to thinking about all the other jobs out there, and the other lives he could be living. The women he could meet and the places he could go with them. He saw how much sewage there was to mash up, and how it never ended, and it felt like the little control cab of the Splasher was closing in on him, and he wanted only to see the sunlight and then he would be happy. This was a dark place he went to, a hopeless place, where he saw only that the day would never end and that tomorrow would never come.

Usually once he got to thinking like that he still had a few hours left of his shift and it wore him out thinking so hard about needing to get out that when he finally did get off work, he was exhausted and didn't care as much as he thought, about the sun, or having his own garden. The sun was already down most of the time anyway, so he went home to his small apartment, looking forward only to his bed, and maybe a hot meal if he had the energy to put something in the microwave.

But on the International Day of Happiness, this did not all happen quite the same way. At about the time he usually started thinking of all the women he could be meeting and the things he could be doing with them, his Splasher lurched. The piston system squealed shrilly. Could be a jam, he thought and throttled down the whirling blade mechanism. He radioed the foreman,

"Possible jam here Mr. Vang, I'm going to get out and take a look."

"Ok, that's fine, don't fall in Hines." Piper laughed politely and opened the hatch. He climbed out carefully. The suit prevented full mobility, and he knew well how often sewage technicians really did fall in. The flood lights lit up the entire cave outside, but the steam and gas coming up from the mass of fermenting waste prevented any practical long distance visibility.

Piper could see a hundred yards in any direction, and there was nothing but steam and sewage. He heard the pumping of a Skimmer off to his left in the direction of shore, and another Splasher somewhere else. He crawled along the hull until he reached the conical spraying valve, its rim coated in the brackish brown of pulverized human waste.

Looking down into the mechanism he saw the fans and behind those, the array of blades which did the actual puree job on the raw sewage. Piper could not tell where the jam was, even with the use of his head lamp, so he stepped back and pulled the lever which lifted and spread open the blades, fan, and cone to make the individual parts accessible in case of a jam. The array swung up out of the muck, dripping lumps, and spread its finger-like blades to reveal the thing that barred their revolutions.

He staggered backwards at the sight of a dripping, half-chewed corpse, crammed between the tines.

"Shit."

"Whatcha got there?" Mr. Vang responded through Piper's headset.

"It's a body, it looks like a dead body, I... I don't know. I won't mess with anything. Maybe we should call the law up on this one." Piper spoke quickly and breathed heavily, he was surprised, but not completely. He sometimes thought that maybe this would happen. There were stories of bodies winding up in the sewage system. He had even slightly hoped on certain slow, tedious shifts that he might be the one to find one. And so there was something strangely exciting in the grotesque discovery.

"Oh god, yeah, I'll make the call. Don't touch anything, just sit tight."

Piper cautiously leaned in and examined the face of the corpse. It was all mangled by the blades, covered in slime, and unidentifiable. He thought it was probably a man's body, but couldn't be positive. There was blood pouring from the gashes and mixing with the sewage. He wondered why it had not been ground up and spit out, then noticed that there was a metal frame surrounding the torso, and this was what hung upon the blades. It was a back brace, the kind used for patients with scoliosis or recovering from sever back injuries. The brace had apparently caused the jam, not the corpse itself. Over the brace, the dead man wore the remnants of a shredded sport coat, with an official looking embroidered patch sewn onto the breast.

Protruding from the breast pocket was a plastic zippered bag with a piece of paper laid flat inside. It had been nearly flung from the pocket in the spinning blades and now hung on the brink of falling to the sewage where it would surely sink. If he could just grab it, he thought, maybe it would help police identify the body. He looked around. The sounds of the other vehicles had stopped.

The sewage reservoir was now a crime scene, not to be disturbed. But there was still no sign of an approaching motor. Quickly, almost without thinking, he leaned out over the gaping blades and plucked the bag from the pocket of the corpse. Rolling back on to his heels he wiped the greenish brown muck off onto his suit, and looked through the smeared plastic.

It was a note, written so that it could be read through the bag without opening it, and in a crazy handwriting, with an almost deliberate change in the style, from a panicked scrawl to formal, clear block lettering. It read:

"Whatever happens,
don't let them say I wasn't happy.
-Garret J. Peterson."

Piper grunted. He began to put the note back into the pocket, the pocket of the Happiest Man in Hennepin County. But the words stuck with him and he paused and took it back, reading the message again. He read it twice more. It slowly began to seem that the note was in fact addressed to him, or at least to whoever found the body. The dead man's note was private, almost intimate, a friend speaking to a friend, though Piper had never met Garret J. Peterson.

All the same Piper wished he had not taken it out. There was no way to explain his tampering with the body. There might be consequences; he was ignorant of the laws. Should he pretend he hadn't seen the note? That might be best. Frantically, he leaned out again and tried to push the bag back in to Garret J. Peterson's breast pocket. In his hurry, he rocked the Splasher and lost his balance. The note fell from his outstretched hand, fluttering to the surface of the sewage where it rocked slowly under. Piper watched helplessly. There was nothing to fish it out with, and no time. He could already hear the hum of the foreman's boat moving toward him through the mist. When he was sure the note was gone he climbed back into the cab, tuned his headphones to the music channel, and waited.

THE PRISONER
BY KEN LUBOLD

"Today TransCorp unveils the latest in brain en-
hancing cranial implants!" Brett Richards stood tall
and handsome at the raised podium, smiling and looking at ease in spite of the heat of the lights focused on
him. The stuffy press room was filled to capacity; reporters from every network and all the major papers
had shown up to hear TransCorp's latest press release.
The global bioengineering firm was the media's dar-
ling, their line of consumer-friendly body and mind
modification devices were well-received by the public
and regarded as status symbols in Hollywood. Brett,
having only recently become vice-president of the company, was still new to the role of spokesman, but his

good looks and easy charm made him a natural. Brett added to the romanticism associated with the company — young, attractive, and successful, he was the face of TransCorp, the embodiment of what the company promised to deliver through its products.

"Intelligence will no longer be a point of contention between people! TransCorp's Mind Spark boosts the synaptic connections in the brain, doubling the power of your own mind! You can be smart, clever, and witty simply by installing the chip into an existing cranial adaptor!" Brett was nearing the end of the prepared speech. Like a minister preaching to his flock, he raised his arms to the air and faced the cameras, preparing for the big finish.

"Hello? Can you hear me?"

Startled, Brett paused in mid-speech. A blank, horrified look eclipsed his perfect smile and he cocked his head to one side, as if listening to someone only he could hear. The rapt audience was silent, watching him expectantly.

Damn! Not now!

Brett tried to pretend he didn't hear the voice in his head, but he had already stumbled and the audience was certain to have noticed. His train of thought derailed, he gaped at the crowd. His spell over them had broken and they were left adrift in the middle of his speech. The seconds ticked by. The crowd grew restless. Someone coughed at the back of the room. Reporters began to grumble, wondering if something was wrong. Brett struggled to recover.

"Mind Spark will be the great equalizer of men and women."

He fought to get back on track, telling himself that the voice was gone and nobody had noticed anything.

"It will negate feelings of inferiority and envy."

The reporters ceased fidgeting as Brett regained their attention. His voice grew stronger as his confidence returned and the crowd quieted as the speech regained momentum.

"A new enlightened age is dawning. We are at the doorway of a new Golden Age of philosophy and science: Mind Spark—brought to you by TransCorp, makers of the Personality Modulation Device!"

"Answer me! Help me!"

The voice returned, but it was too late. Drowned out by the cheering crowd, Brett found it easy to ignore.

Brett stepped down from the podium and entered an ocean of congratulations, engulfed by politicians and reporters who sought to clasp his hand and clap him on the back. The odd lapse in the speech was forgotten.

"You cut the speech a little short. Is everything okay, Mr. Richards?"

Donna, his assistant, met him at the far end of the room and walked with him out to the limo. She was young, competent, and extremely attractive. Brett had been trying to get her to go home with him since he first became vice-president. Unfortunately, she seemed to have some moral barrier against sleeping with her boss.

"Everything's fine, just thought I'd speed things up a bit, that's all." They got into the limo together and Brett took a small amount of pleasure in watching Donna's skirt ride up a bit higher on her thigh as she sat down.

"The press conference went well overall I think." She ignored his leering at her legs.

"Why won't you answer me!"

The voice returned so suddenly that Brett jerked in surprise, his smirk vanishing. Donna inspected him with one slender eyebrow raised.

"...yes. Yes, I think it went very well." He smoothed back his hair with one hand, trying to appear casual.

"Are you sure you're okay Mr. Richards?"

"Yes, of course I am. Just...drained, that's all. Say, what are you doing for dinner tonight Donna?"

The voice stayed quiet for the rest of the ride, allowing Brett to continue his flirtations with Donna, who pretended not to understand his propositions.

It took a little practice to learn to ignore the voice. Occasionally he would mistake it for one of the people around him, especially if he was busy entertaining clients or distracted by a pretty girl. The voice was always plaintive, not hurt exactly, but confused and panicky, like a man who had been buried alive.

Sleeping was the hardest part. It was very difficult to drift off with a voice pleading with you at the edge of your hearing. It wouldn't be so bad if you could just locate the source of the voice, like if it was a kid who had hurt himself in the apartment across the way, or even a guy beating his wife. At least then there'd be a cause, something you could point to and say "there, that's where that terrible sound is coming from." Simply naming and understanding the phenomenon would make it much more bearable. Once you understood the cause you could rectify it — pick the kid up and slap a band-aid on him, or call the cops on the asshole who liked using his fists. Unfortunately, it wasn't like that. There was no origin of the voice, at least none that could be found, so he had no indication of how to stop it.

Brett had begun hearing the voice nearly two months ago. He had been under a lot of stress at the time, having just landed the vice-president position, a high-profile, high-responsibility, and most importantly, high-paying job. There had been fierce competition for the promotion, a lot of back-stabbing and under-handed dealings, but he had come out on top. So when he first began hearing mysterious disembodied voices he wrote it off as a natural reaction to stress and anxiety.

In the beginning, he would ask people around him if they heard the voice too, but he quickly learned that was a mistake. Asking the guy standing next to you in the cramped elevator "Hey, do you hear somebody crying for help?" never seemed to come off as anything but crazy. It didn't help that no one else heard the voice.

Ever.

Not once did another person perk up, saying "My God! Do you hear that? It sounds like someone is trapped somewhere!" As far as he knew, he was the only person who could hear it, which was annoying because he was far too busy to be having a psychotic episode.

Brett wasn't the kind of guy who typically heard voices. True, he was still living in the same crappy apartment he had before getting the promotion, but that was only until he closed on his house. He made excellent money with the new job, wore hand-made suits, drove a nice car... He wasn't in a committed relationship but he knew a few different girls who were always willing to go out on a Friday or Saturday night and stick around until the next morning. As the vice-president of TransCorp, the largest neural engineering firm in the nation, he held a prestigious place in high society. His life in the spotlight made it imperative that he maintain an impeccable façade. If anyone knew he was hearing voices it would cause a major scandal and his career would never recover. So he carried on with his life and tried to ignore the voice in his head.

The limo dropped Brett and Donna off at the office where they picked up their own cars. Unsuccessful once again at convincing Donna to come home with him, Brett drove home alone. His anger at the press conference was exacerbated by his failure to seduce Donna and he raged at himself while he drove. The conference had been a close one. A major publicity event with reporters from all the TV networks and he had very nearly come out looking like a fool. Staring vacantly into space, mouth agape like an idiot. It was unacceptable. He was successful, powerful, loved and admired; he could conquer anything. He could over-come any obstacle. The notion that a man like himself could be intimidated by a phantom was preposterous. He would not allow himself to be distracted by any-thing, especially not a disembodied voice that only he could hear! He couldn't allow the situation to contin-ue. Sooner or later people would begin to notice.

Brett parked outside his drab apartment complex, and stomped up the stairs to his third floor apartment, still fuming. The building wasn't awful, but it served as a lingering reminder of his life before being named vice president. The factory-white walls and tacky car-peting of the halls fueled his anger at the phantom voice. Reaching his door, he unlocked it, stepped in-side, and slammed it behind him. He had ignored the voice for too long. Hoping that it was a product of stress and that it would go away on its own wasn't working. He would confront the voice once and for all and browbeat it into submission.

Throwing his coat onto a chair and pulling off his tie, he raged against the invisible entity that dared to mock him.

"Get out of my head! I'm done with you! Do you hear me?!"

Silence. No response from the voice.

"You're there, I know you're there! I want you gone!" He kicked over the chair. He wandered around the apartment looking at the ceiling, inspecting every corner as if he would discover the voice hiding in a cobweb.

"You...you can you hear me?! For God's sake help me!" Hope filled the voice as it begged for help from the man that had ignored it for two months.

"Yes, I can hear you! That's the problem! Get out of my life!"

Brett had no intention of prolonging the confrontation. The less time spent talking to himself the better. The voice was that of a weak man, frightened and helpless. Brett knew the best way to deal with such a person was to intimidate them as quickly and completely as possible, until they abandoned all demands and surrendered.

"Who are you? Where am I?" Hope turned to bewilderment as the apparition was confronted by Brett's

imperious anger.

"I don't know where you are and I don't care! I'm Brett Richards, the vice-president of TransCorp Global Industries, and I demand that you get out of my head!"

Silence for a moment, and Brett felt a thrill at so easily overcoming the bizarre specter. And then it spoke again, stunned and quiet.

"...that's impossible. That doesn't make sense!"

"None of this makes sense! But I don't care anymore! I'm a powerful and important person and I will not be subject to hearing voices!" He punched the wall for emphasis, bruising his knuckles and enraging himself further.

"No. I mean, I'm Brett Richards." Diminished by Brett's outbursts, the voice was as meek as a frightened kitten. But it spoke with conviction.

"What? What did you just say?"

"I said I'm Brett Richards. I work at TransCorp. But I'm not the vice-president."

"You're lying. You can't be Brett Richards because that's me. Do you hear me?! I'm Brett Richards!" Rather than being confused by this identity conflict, Brett only grew angrier.

How dare another person, especially this abomination, claim to be him? It wasn't even a person, just a phantom voice, words without a body, a shadow, a nothing. He was Brett Richards, his existence proved it. His post as vice-president of the most powerful corporation in the world, his car, the bank account with his name on it, his apartment, his prestige — these were the things that defined Brett Richards, the things that he had fought to earn.

"You are NOT me! You are nothing, a nobody! You're just a ghost! Nobody even hears you!" Brett charged across the apartment like a mad bull, tossing furniture out of his way. He destroyed his possessions both to intimidate the voice and to affirm his existence — he could tear his home apart, demolish all of his belongings, and tomorrow he could replace them, put everything back the way it was. He was a dervish of destruction, smashing a glass-topped coffee table with a thrown dining room chair, kicking over bookshelves, overturning an armchair...

"You are not me because I am not you! People pay attention to me! They listen to what I have to say! They hang on my every word! Power and influence! That's what I am! What Brett Richards is!" He upended the couch and it came crashing down to the floor, startling the neighbors in the apartment below who began to pound on the ceiling.

"Shut up, up there! Are you crazy!? We're gonna call the goddamn cops if you don't shut up!" Brett heard the muffled voices of his neighbors through the floor boards.

He dropped the book he was about to throw at the window and tried to calm down. He told himself to relax, to pull it together. He could make it through this. He could get through anything.

"It doesn't matter what you have or what you break. I AM Brett Richards, and I don't think you can make me leave". The voice was quiet, subdued, but with a spark of defiance.

Brett felt hot anger rising up his spine, threatening to overwhelm him again, but he controlled it. He hated that whiny voice, challenging him as if it were his equal. But despite what it said, he would find a way to get rid of it.

The next morning, he showered and dressed quickly. He raced to work, weaving in and out of lanes, always trying to get one more car ahead. Donna, as usual, greeted him at the office. Despite being preoccupied, he couldn't help but notice the tight sweater she wore.

"Good morning, Mr. Richards. The coffee just finished brewing, if you'd like some." She smiled at him, ignoring his eyes on her chest. "Ah, no thanks Donna, but I need you to cancel my morning appointments."

"All of them? Remember, you're supposed to meet with Senator Buchold today." Donna was surprised — Brett had never skipped a meeting.

"Yes, I know, but he's going to have to wait."

"Is something wrong?" Genuine concern in her voice — she really was a great assistant. If only she would sleep with him.

"I need you to make an appointment for me with Dr. Carver this morning."

"Dr. Carver?" She stopped there. She didn't ask

why he wanted to meet with the company psychia-
trist. TransCorp worked its employees very hard, but
they received numerous compensations, including free
counseling to deal with the inevitable stress of the job.

"Yes, an appointment with Dr. Carver, as soon as he
is available." Brett kept his voice level, not wanting to
alarm his loyal assistant.

"Okay. I'll set it up."

The good doctor managed to find an open hour
for Brett with little trouble. Actually, Brett knew that
Dr. Carver was always booked solid weeks in advance
and must have cancelled or rearranged a number of
appointments to fit him in, but he didn't care, that was
his right as vice-president.

The doctor's office was paneled in dark wood and
smelled of ink and old paper. Dr. Carver was a small
man, dark and hairy, with eyebrows like autumn cater-
pillars. But he was warm and engaging, and his hand-
shake was friendly and firm without being aggressive.

"Come in Mr. Richards, I'm happy to see you!" He
gestured Brett to take one of the comfy chairs across
from his desk.

"Thank you, Doctor. I appreciate you seeing me on
such short notice."

"Nonsense! More than happy to see you! Now,
how can I help you?" They both took their seats and regarded each other across the beautiful mahogany desk.

"Well, I've been under a lot of stress lately." Brett

began slowly, gauging the Doctor's reaction. He had thought this conversation through last night and decided to proceed cautiously. If the doctor showed any alarm or anxiety about Brett's revelation he would pull back, reel in the conversation and extricate himself. Better to live with the voice than to damage his reputation and career.

"Well, that's understandable. You've only been vice-president for, what, two months?"

"Yes, two months. And it has been very stressful — I'm sure it's just the stress. I can handle stress, that's not the problem. But I've also been experiencing some... well, I guess you'd say hallucinations." Brett chuckled a bit, to show the doctor it wasn't a big deal and that he wasn't too concerned.

"Well, that's not unusual. Many people experience strange visions or noises during periods of intense stress or as a result of sleep deprivation." Brett was relieved that the doctor's manner was still relaxed.

"Yes, that's exactly what I mean. A lot of stress and not enough sleep, I'm sure that explains it. It's just kind of irritating, you know, to be hearing this voice and you can't shut it up? I even had an argument with it, can you believe that? I argued with this voice inside my head, it was crazy, he kept saying that he was me, that I wasn't myself!" Encouraged by the doctor's understanding, Brett relieved himself of his secret. It felt good, to finally be able to talk to someone about the voice, knowing that there was a rational explanation.

"You had an argument with this voice, you say? And it insisted that it was you?" The doctor had suddenly become serious, his smile had faded and he began to peer at Brett with concern."Well, yes, but—like you said—I'm sure it's just stress. Stress and sleep deprivation, it would happen to anybody, like you were saying."

Oh shit, what was going on? Had he said too much?

"Okay. Sure, that's probably all it is. But given the work that the company does I've got to ask—just to cover all the bases so to speak—what is the implant you're currently wearing?" The doctor was all smiles again, but Brett could tell he was still a bit concerned. But what was this about implants? He didn't wear any implants. TransCorp had no rules against their employees making use of their products, in fact they encouraged their more visible team members—like Brett—to wear them in public, but Brett secretly disliked the things. To his mind, TransCorp's personality modification implants were crutches for the weak, tools that losers used to compensate for their shortcomings. Brett was contemptuous of the implants and those who used them.

"I don't know what you mean—I'm not wearing any implants. Never have."

"Well, I don't mean to contradict you, but I noticed an implant when you first came into my office. I can just see it...right here." The doctor spoke gently, tilting his head and tapping a finger at the base of his skull.

Brett reached a hesitant hand around to the back of

his head and was surprised to find the end of a small cranial implant poking out from under his hair. Touching the implant triggered a memory, one that had been hidden away and denied since its creation. A memory that he shared, but had never made.

He remembered visiting a company doctor a little over two months ago, wanting to get a leg-up on the competition for the vice-presidential nomination. He had a personality modifier installed, a confidence program to bolster his interview skills and impress his supervisors with a new force of character. But that wasn't quite right...he didn't have a personality modifier installed, he was the personality modifier. And the voice in his head was the old self, his weak other-self that lacked charisma and confidence, a flawed personality that was incapable of winning the promotion on his own, an obsolete fragment that he dominated and subsumed as the inheritor of the flesh they both inhabited.

Sharing the same brain, the voice experienced the memory at the same time and railed against the traitor that had enslaved it.

"You can't do this to me! You have no right! You have to let me go!"

Except he could do it—he was doing it. As long as he left the implant in, he was in control. And wasn't it better this way? He had won the vice-presidency; he had money, power, influence, and women—what else could he possibly want?

"You can't leave me imprisoned like this, trapped in my own head! You're not me...you're an impostor!"

Brett smiled and directed his thoughts at his former self. "I don't know why you're so angry. You were the one that installed me, remember? I'm not an impostor, I'm an improvement. You should be grateful! I've created a better life for us, one you were incapable of achieving on your own. I am your successor, a natural evolution."

"I won't let you do this. You can't just lock me away. I'll always be here, a voice inside your mind."

"Yes, that's all you are: a whisper in the dark. You're incapable of anything else. And I can learn to ignore you, now that I know what you are."

"Is everything okay, Mr. Richards?" The doctor again, concerned now.

"Oh, yes, everything's fine! Can you believe I actually forgot I had this implant in? Silly thing, it's just a language translator, lets me understand Japanese. Forgot all about it!" Chuckle a bit. Flash him a sheepish grin. He's already relaxing.

"Ah, of course. I understand. I know many of the senior members routinely wear translators. Okay... well, why don't you tell me a bit more about this voice you've been hearing?"

"Tell him. Tell him about me, about what you've done. Tell him that you've imprisoned your own mind!"

"Well, you know, I'm sure it's just stress. After talking about it for a bit I realize how little sleep I've been getting, and all the work we've been doing lately... It's just been crazy! But I feel much better just having talked about it!"

"Are you sure, Mr Richards? I mean, these things should be monitored, they don't always just go away on their own."

"I'll come back if it persists, but I really think I'll be better now. You've really helped me to look at my life, you know, get things in perspective so I can relax and slow down a bit. I don't think I would have been able to do it without you!" Let him know how important he is, how his advice was crucial; make him feel special.

"Well, alright, but I want you to come back straight away if you have any more trouble, okay?" The doctor was back to his role of caring parent, his fears forgotten.

"Okay. I even promise to make an appointment next time!" They both laughed, and Brett excused himself from the doctor's office.

"You won't get away with this. You can't keep me like this forever."

"Oh? Why not? What are you going to do about it?"

Brett continued laughing as he walked back to his office, his sexy assistant, his money and prestige.

BICYCLOPOLIS
BY KEN AVIDOR

BICYCLOPOLIS

JOURNAL OF MY JOURNEY TO THE FORMER MINNESOTA
By Percival Flodge*

My journey to the former Minnesota is the first of any European since the United States Collapsed seventy years ago.

Thank You Thank You Thank You Have a Nice Day

Minnesotans were thought to be extinct until last year when a message in a bottle was found by fishermen tied to a pole on the rocky shore of Hudson's Bay.

*Assisted by K. Avidor

I embarked on a sailing ship with a sturdy bicycle for the long trip. After a short voyage, I disembarked at the spot designated in the letter. I was met by my guide.

Norway
Scotland
Iceland
Ireland
Greenland
Sea of Storms (Atlantic)
Canada

The ice-free Polar route

Her name was Sara

We bicycled south through a choking haze from Hundreds of peat fires in the dried out tundra.

North Ameri Expeditio

HUDSON BAY

Northern Desert

Superior Salt flats

Metroria

Bicyclopolis

LANDFILL KINGDOMS of METRORIA

Isanti-chisago

Oak Grove Anoka BETHEL

Lindenteiser Woodlake WDE Pine Lake

French Lake Hopkins Johnson

Flying Cloud Washington Cap

Louisville Freeway

Dakhue

Over a campfire, Sara described the route we would take across the former Canada now a desert. The next day. We biked across the Superior Salt flats.

After several days bicycling, we arrived in Metroria. Before the collapse, Metroria was called the Metro Area of the Twin Cities, an automobile-dependant suburban region. Metroria is now a desolate wasteland littered with the rusting hulks of useless vehicles and the crumbling ruins of shopping malls and concrete highways.

The Obeasts

Obese Minnesotans were once common but few survived the collapse. Those that did survive, gorged on toxic garbage in the landfills, mutating into huge, lumbering beasts.

I observed wild obeasts being roped and tamed by "velogueros". They sold the tamed obeasts to the Metrorians.

Faith and Religion in Metroria

Minnesotans plunged into a deep despair in the wake of the Collapse. Many chose to cling to the useless remnants of their doomed technocentric civilsation.

The loss of their personal automobiles was felt most acutely.

The widespread longing for a return to an autocentric era encouraged the creation of messianic car-worshipping cults.

Knights of Metroria

A typical knight with his mount.

Tall Skirmish bike

A Joust

A Metrorian "Signifier" with a Standard of logos.

Weapons recycled from an abundant supply of scrap iron.

leaf-spring crossbow

Metrorian Sword

rebar pike

I observed a Metrorian army prepare to lay siege to a fortified City.

55

Metrorian Siege Warfare

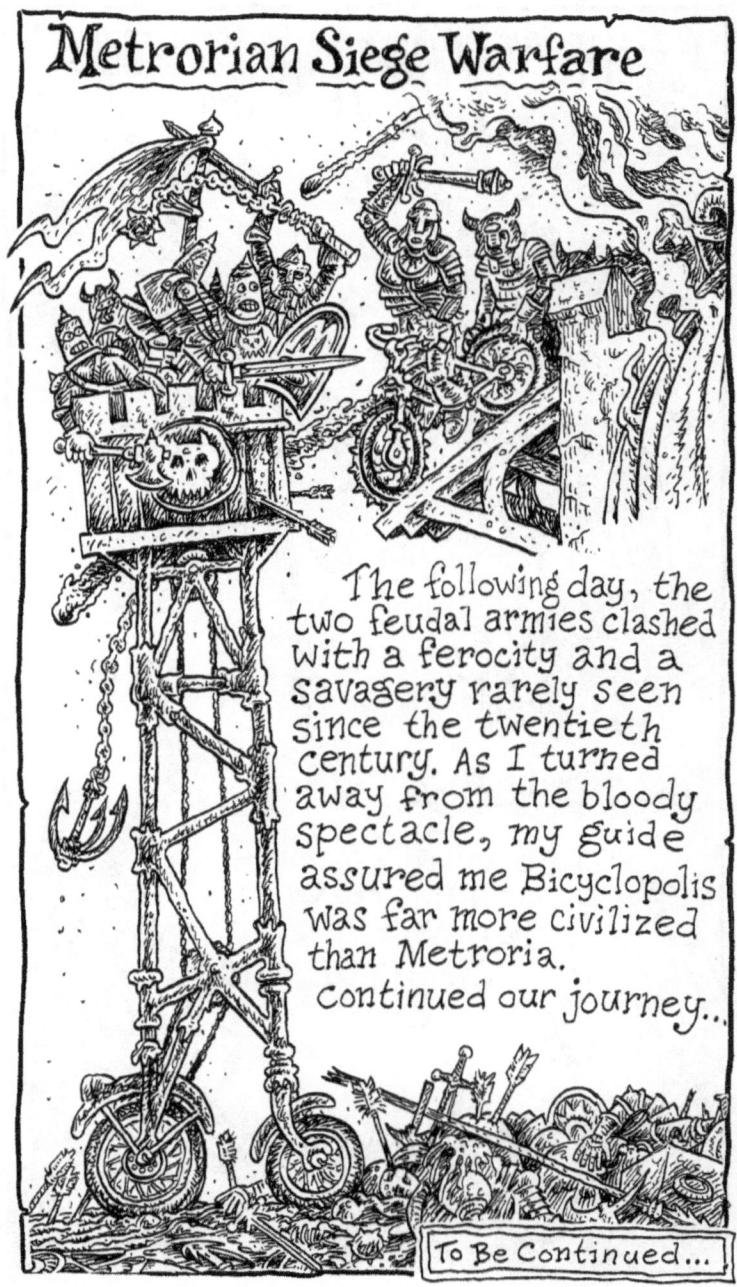

The following day, the two feudal armies clashed with a ferocity and a savagery rarely seen since the twentieth century. As I turned away from the bloody spectacle, my guide assured me Bicyclopolis was far more civilized than Metroria. continued our journey...

To Be Continued...

WHAT'S FOR DINNER
BY AARON M. WILSON

1.
Double Dog Dare, Tater Tots, and Brau Brothers' Pale Ale

After taking a long look in the birthday mirror, Penny was disgusted. In the mirror, she saw rolls of fat that sagged around her waist and under her arms so her elbows were almost parallel with her shoulders. She saw an overly round face supported by two, almost three chins. As she stood in front of the mirror scrutinizing her body, she felt the muscles in her back and legs twitch and her heart straining to push blood to her extremities. The worst part of looking into the mirror was that she could see out into the lonely living room over her shoulder. She could hear the TV. The Twins were playing the Sox. Even though she didn't know even one of the Twins personally, she counted each and everyone of them a friend. The Twins were her only friends. Thinking about the Twins and especially Joe Mauer, she opened a bathroom sink drawer next to the mirror and retrieved her dildo. But she caught sight of herself in the mirror again and put the vibrator away. She was tired of spending her birthdays alone, at home with a pint or two of Sebastian Joe's ice cream. Thoroughly depressed, she pulled on her clothes and her coat. She was going to walk down the street to the Bulldog. "Enough," she thought and turned off the TV, "I'm going for a drink and a hot dog."

In her fat pants, gray sweats with the name of her alma mater down one leg, white running shoes, and a Twins baseball cap, Penny picked the table closest to the kitchen and farthest from everyone else in the restaurant. She leaned the back of her chair against the wall, making sure that she could see the game: Twins 2, Sox 4, top of the fourth inning. Penny, showing her frustration with the Twins' scoring ability, grabbed the bill of her cap, and it swatted loudly on the table.

A skinny waitress in a tight midriff exposing t-shirt hustled over. "Sorry for the wait." She laid down a set of silverware wrapped in a black napkin and both the food and drink menus.

"What are you drinking tonight?"

Ignoring the menus Penny ordered her usual, "Brau Brothers' Pale Ale, and I'll have the Double Dog Dare."

"Sure." The waitress pulled out her pad of order tickets from her apron. "What two dogs you want?"

"A Chicago and a Homewrecker."

"Sorry, the Double Dog Dare doesn't include The Homewrecker because it is a full half-pound. If I can make a recommendation…"

"It's my birthday." Penny pushed the menus toward the edge of the table as if daring the waitress to interrupt her. "I'm thirty and feeling a little self-destructive, just make it work. I'll pay the extra."

"You got it." The waitress scribbled a couple of notes on the ticket as she walked the couple feet over to the kitchen window.

Penny went back to watching the Twins. They were down another run. The Sox must have scored while she was ordering. Before the next Sox batter stepped up to home plate, her beer slid towards her over the table.

"Brau Brothers' Pale," said a tall, muscular man with a lumberjack beard and tattooed arms, "for the birthday girl."

Penny nodded and took a sip. "That's the stuff."

"It's a slow night." He waved his arm indicating the empty bar. "Can I join you for a few minutes?"

Penny pushed the brim of her cap up and took another sip off her beer. The foamy head ran between her fingers and down the side of the cold glass.

"As long as you don't spoil the party."

"Aren't many Twins fans left." He took the seat next to Penny on her side of the table. He looked up at the screen. "Ever since the Twins won the World Series in 2051 because of that bad umpire call…"

"Yeah, yeah. Everyone's a critic these days." Penny scooted her chair away from the bartender towards the corner, which afforded a little more elbowroom.

"Name's Parker." He extended his hand, green, orange, and blue lines formed a coy fish that wrapped around his wrist and looked as if was swimming up the underside of arm.

Penny took his hand. "Penny."

"What's your interest in the Twins?" He looked away from Penny and at the screen. "They have had the worst record in the league for five years now."

"I live a few blocks from here." Penny wasn't in the mood for chatting. She wanted to drink, and she wanted to drink alone. It was her birthday. She shouldn't have to entertain on her birthday. She should be allowed to have a drink, eat a couple of hot dogs, and watch the Twins lose again in peace.

"The Twins are here. I'm here. They're my team."

Parker nodded. "That's how I feel about them too." He pulled at his beard with his left hand exposing a tattoo of elaborately drawn letters and numbers.

Penny wasn't in the mood to flirt, but not being able to read his tattoo frustrated her. He had decided to join her, so he should be open to a few questions. She just hoped that he didn't get the impression that she was interested.

"Ugh," she thought, "whom am I kidding? He's hot. I'm not." Shaking her head she said, "Okay. I can't read your tattoo."

He held his arm up. "You mean this one?"

"Yeah, that one. I can see that it's a list." She pointed at the numbers, "One, two, three, but I can't make out what it is a list of?"

"Food rules."

"Food rules?"

"Yeah, I came across a little book of basic food rules when I was at the U in an introduction to environmental science."

Penny cracked a smile for the first time that day. "Science? What happened?"

"I dropped out." Parker shrugged his shoulder. "I wanted to be a writer." He ran his hand through his hair. "Novels. The general courses at the U killed the experience for me. Besides, I don't need to pay anyone thousands of dollars to learning something that I can research for free at the Public Library."

Penny pointed at the tattoo again and took a long pull on her beer. She thought, "Oh no. What did I get myself into? I just want to know what his tattoo says. It's my birthday!"

"In that science class, we learned about some guy named Michael Pollan. He's written several books, but the one that changed my life was Food Rules: An Eater's

Manual. So, I tattooed his three basic rules on my arm."

"Are you going to make me ask?" Penny snuck a peek at the Twins score. They were down another run.

Parker pointed to the number one. "Eat food." Next, he pointed to number two. "Mostly plants." Finally, at number three. "Not too much."

"That's it?" Penny unabashedly snorted beer back into her glass. "You got to be kidding me. If it were that easy, everyone would be like you and her." Penny's upper lip curled, and she pointed at her waitress.

Parker laughed. "Jennifer is skinny, but I bet she starves herself to look that way." Parker stood up. "Look, my break's over. Thirsty people can't wait." He stopped and turned around to face Penny again. "You're right. Pollan's rules are more complicated, but they work. Flirting, he lifted his shirt exposing the tight muscles of his stomach. "I'd tried to lose weight before, but nothing worked. Once I addressed the source of my weight problem, the food I was eating, everything changed. We're nothing more than complex machines, and when I maintained my machine with artificial, high calorie, highly processed foods, I gained weight. When I started reading labels and buying locally grown produce, I lost weight. Best of all, I wasn't hungry."

Penny looked at the Double Dog Dare that her waitress, Jennifer, had just set down. She'd opted to substitute the potato chips with tater tots. She loved tater tots. The Twins were down another run. She looked at her hotdogs. "Damn it!" She looked over at the bar. Parker was flipping glasses and filling them. "What right does he have," Penny thought, "to tell me how to eat. I'm celebrating my birthday here."

Jennifer still hovering nearby asked, "What's wrong? Can I get you another drink?"

Penny didn't want to be chatty, but she spoke up anyway. "Look at this. Look at me." She pushed the dogs across the table.

"Our dogs aren't the best if you're health conscious, but they are a great treat." Jennifer moves in closer and leans one elbow on the table. "We make 'em fresh once a week with top quality meat. I can tell you all about it if you like."

Penny nodded.

"Sure." Jennifer stood up, pulled the gum out of her mouth, and held it between her thumb and index fingers. "We use free-range animals local to Minnesota or Wisconsin. No hormones. It's good stuff."

"Is it good for me?" Penny snuck a tatter tot.

"If you're going to eat meat, sure. It's better than feed-lot." Jennifer looked over her shoulder. "I got to go. Enjoy."

Penny wondered if she'd dropped into an episode of the Twilight Zone. Who were these people who thought so much about their food. Well, she couldn't let the food go to waste. Maybe she'd get one of them wrapped up for lunch tomorrow.

2.

Ground Bison, Asparagus, and City Tap Water

"What?" Penny stood in the kitchen watching her double boiler. She had a pound of locally grown asparagus steaming that would be ready in five minutes. However, she was angry with Parker. She was going to be hungry again tonight because he failed to read the label on the bison.

Parker plated a bison burger on both of their plates, which included locally baked buns of local wheat, local spring onions, and local heirloom tomatoes.

"Pen, they're local."

"Local's not good enough." Penny lifted her shirt. Her stomach was soft and slightly round. She'd lost a lot of weight, but she felt she had a long way to go yet. "Those growth hormones keep me fat." She opened the lid to check on the asparagus. They were just starting to be tender. "I won't eat it."

"Come on, Pen. Be reasonable." Parker put her arms around her waist. "Just a few months ago, you didn't care about any of this local and organic stuff."

Penny pushed him away. "Now I do."

"It's cooked. It's ready."

"This isn't the first time you've failed to check the label." Penny pulled the pot off the stove and lifted the top tier off the boiling water. "I've about had it."

"What do you mean, 'had it'?" Parker stood between her and their plates.

Penny pulled a clean plate out of the cupboard. She dumped the cooked asparagus on the plate. "I'm not eating your trash." She moved to the small two-person table wedged in the corner between the stove and the apartment door.

"Ever since you got your tattoo, you've been unreasonable." Parker picked up the other burger and put it on his plate. "You won't shop anywhere but The Wedge, and they're the most expensive store in the Twin Cities." He put his plate down on the table hard enough that their two water glasses sloshed. "We can't afford to shop there all the time. Didn't you catch Pollan's section on do as much as you can when you can? We can't. We don't make enough." He sat in the red chair nearest to the door.

"We can." Penny finished chewing. "And we will only eat local-organic food that is in season."

"Pen."

"I've been called back for a second interview." Penny pointed her fork at Parker. "When I'm a Dagger Doll, I'll have enough money." She stabbed a couple skinny spears and bit off the flowers.

Parker shook his head. "I can't believe we're fighting over food.

"I can." Penny took a sip of water. "There's nothing more important than food issues."

Parker pushed his burgers toward the center of the

table. They looked artful against the yellow painted tabletop.

"More important than me?"

Penny let her arms hang and her shoulders sag. She had known that Parker was bad news ever since their first date. He seemed to be into her because she was over weight. He was a real chubby-chaser. This wasn't the first time she'd thought he'd brought home hormone-filled meat. He wanted her fat. She could see it in his eyes when he looked at her naked. At first he'd been all over her. Now, after she'd converted her eating habits and shed almost fifty pounds, he didn't stay over as many nights a week. When he did stay, they didn't always have sex.

"Well?" Parker asked. "Is your diet more important than me?"

Penny simply said, "Yes."

3.
Picked Potatoes, Jerked Beef, and Irradiated Water

Penny, armed with three large cotton bags, entered the grocery store at the corner of W. 22nd Street and S. Lyndale Ave. She put her bags into a green double-decker grocery cart that was no more than two hand baskets, one suspended a few inches above the other. After claiming a cart and relinquishing her bags, Penny removed her mittens and her knit cap, letting her blond and purple dreadlocks tumble past her shoulders, and opened her puffy pink parka.

Even though it was cold today, the sun was out. The sun's deadly rays shone through the tinted glass windows facing west out onto Lyndale Ave. For a flash second, she remembered last week's televised surgeon general's warning about this spring's unsafe UV levels: skin would likely burn in under five minutes of exposure and blindness would likely follow more than thirty minutes of unprotected exposure. No causes or explanations were given, just the warning. The Star-Tribune had tried to follow up, but their articles amounted to nothing more than hearsay and conjecture. They ran an interesting piece a few days later about an influx of homeless and poor to the ER reporting sudden onset optic neuropathy. Penny thought she'd better leave her protective goggles on until she was deeper into the store's isles. At home, Penny had painted over her windows to match the adjacent walls. She still had hopes, when she could spare a few dollars on something besides food, to blow-up a couple photographs of the view she used to have from her windows and fix them to the painted-up windows to lessen the impression she was living in an eggshell-white box. Despite having to wear goggles, Penny remained upbeat and pushed her cart further into the store. She loved shopping for groceries here.

The grocery store was warm. Clerks in short-sleeves

and ratty jeans covered by black or green-pocketed aprons re-stocked the shelves of preserved food. Nothing could be locally grown and harvested near the Twin Cities this time of year. It might be early spring, but the ground was still frozen solid in May this far north and would likely still be implantable on the first of June.

Food costs were up everywhere, which if Penny stopped to think about the cost of shopping exclusively at The Wedge Co-op, she'd might, for a second anyway, consider buying groceries somewhere else. However, the prospect of buying food from a traditional grocery store frightened her and should frighten anyone with even a fulcrum of commonsense. A while back, after joining the Co-op, Penny had joined The Wedge, bought a membership, and committed herself to only eating food bought there. If she couldn't find something at The Wedge Co-op, she would do without it. Subsequently, her life had changed.

Penny hung her parka on the back of her grocery cart after warming up a bit. She sported a black three-quarter sleeve fitted women's t-shirt emblazoned with the pink dagger logo of the Dagger Dolls rollergirl team, one of the four Minnesota Rollergirl teams that called the Legendary Roy Wilkins Auditorium, in Saint Paul, their home. Her professional rollergirl name was printed in pink letters across the back of her shoulders, Penny Slots.

As if she were grooving to an internal house music beat, she danced through the organic produce isles, labeled with country of origin. The prices were exorbitant. Apples from Chile and Argentina cost twenty-two dollars per pound. There were only a few places left in the world with growing seasons long enough for most fruits and leafy-green vegetables, and they were mostly in the Southern Hemisphere. Expensive-to-produce photovoltaic cells had solved the global reliance on fossil fuel too late to stop the climate shift of 2025. Cold climates, like Minnesota, had gotten colder, while warm climates, like the equator, had gotten warmer, and the combination of the two had been devastating to farmers and anyone who liked to eat.

Instead, Penny shopped the preserve isles, which was really the majority of the store. The Wedge, staying on the cutting edge of organics and food trends, had converted most of the store into what would have resembled grandma's cellar in the early 1900's. Rows and rows of mason jars containing jams and preserves and pickled tomatoes, cucumbers, and even asparagus lined the shelves. Everything that could be vacuum-packed, canned, or frozen without the aid of harsh chemicals or the addition of too much sodium was how The Wedge attracted its customers. Bison, chicken, and pig, raised locally was still available, but meat was a luxury Penny could only rarely afford now that she would only buy and eat food humanely treated and fed a natural diet of grasses grown without the aid of pesticides and herbicides. Once a week, on Wednesday's, she'd buy a steak no larger than the palm of her hand and no thicker than one of Parker's published novellas. She loved his writing. Too bad it hadn't worked out between them. He just wasn't as committed to eating exclusively what could be purchased from The Wedge, and he still worked at the Bulldog.

The Bulldog's food was bought locally, and they did make their own tater tots fresh from real potatoes, but they weren't certified organic. Organic mattered to Penny. If she could, she'd buy local-organic. If she couldn't buy local organic, she'd fork over the money for organics grown elsewhere in the United States. If organics grown in the United States weren't available, she'd buy organics from another country. And if organics weren't available at all, she'd try to go without or in extreme cases buy conventional-local, and her selection process would start over again. Parker had not been committed enough.

At one point in her food journey, Penny had shopped differently. Buying local food, as Michael Pollan had explained it, was more important than buying organic. He had said to watch the food miles, but that just wasn't possible now, and the alternative to buying organic was horrifying to Penny.

Penny read the newspaper everyday and listened to Minnesota Public Radio instead of watching TV. She saved all food related stories. She couldn't believe what was going on with conventionally produced foods. Scientists were involved at the genetic level trying to reengineer our basic sources of food, mainly the big four: corn, wheat, rice, and soy, to grow bigger and faster so that they could be grown in places like Iowa again.

Since she had started scrutinizing her food, she had discovered that genetically modifying food wasn't a new idea. However, some of the things these new crops could resist, pests of all kinds, blight, frozen soil, and harsh UV radiation, made her ask what consuming these plants over time would do to a human. Penny had looked, but no long-term studies had been conducted, and one of the chemicals being used to treat these genetically modified crops was an atrazine derivative. High levels of atrazine in river and lake water in the early 2000's was known to cause sexual reproductive issues in male frogs and small mouth bass. Males in both species when studied were found to have produced female ovum instead of sperm, effectively castrating them. There were no known cases of human males producing ovum, but why would anyone take the chance?

There were worse and more common ailments from eating conventionally produced genetically modified foods. The one that worried Penny the most was having unexpected allergic reaction to a food spliced with peanut DNA. Penny was deathly allergic to peanuts, and peanut DNA was commonly used to boost production of plants like tomatoes. Peanut plants produced hundreds of nuts per plant, a highly valued trait that scientists liked to tout as the trait that will save the world from going hungry.

While Penny was looking through a shelf of black beans, in the bean and potato isle, a man with black hair dusted with gray came up to Penny. He didn't look like a typical Wedge customer. He kept looking around the store as if lost, and he squinted at the origin of production labels as if they'd jump off the shelves and bite him as he walked down the aisles. As he approached Penny, he pulled out his hand-sized computer. "Penny Slots, can I get a picture with you for my daughter? She's a big fan of the Dagger Dolls."

He must have seen her on the street and followed her into the store. "Sure." Penny pushed her cart to the side of the aisle. She shook out her hair a little more, separating rope-like stands from each other. "Just a second." Penny pulled off her black Dagger Doll sweats off over her shoes and knotted her t-shirt above her belly button.

Nervously, looking around the store, the fan said, "Please, that's not necessary."

"I worked hard for this body." Penny pulled up her knee high socks and cocked her hip to the left.

"Now, who's going to take our picture?" Penny slipped into her role as Penny Slots too easily these days. She wondered how much of plain-old Penny was left. Ever since the Women's Flat Track Association had let corporate sponsorship into the sport, girls like Penny often went pro for as long as their bodies held up under the stress of being body checked on roller-skates. One drawback to sponsorship, not that they had to wear company logo or star in commercials, was that they were required to stay in character while out in public. Staying in character meant taking pictures and bringing the attitude, it also meant that Penny only existed in her apartment these days.

"Here." He pushed a couple mason cans filled with potatoes back on the shelf, and he placed his computer in their spot. Next, he set the camera function for ten seconds, which it counted down in a clear movie voice-over voice.

They centered themselves in the viewfinder by watching themselves in the computers display. He stood against the other side of the aisle while Penny Slots posed in front of him.

Watching herself contort her flat stomach so she could see muscled lines arch around her belly into her tight Minnesota Rollergirl briefs, Penny flexed her tattooed arms and pushed out her breasts. When Penny heard the camera snap the picture, she reached for it and looked at herself. She thought, I looked completely different three years ago. I was someone else three years ago, but now I'm Penny Slots. Aloud to her fan's father, Penny said, "Here you go. I hope she likes it."

Penny pulled on her sweats and untied her shirt. She was going to back to shopping when the fan's father stopped her.

"My daughter has always liked your tattoos. Can

you tell me about the one on the underside of your left arm?" He held up his computer. "Can I film your answer for her? She won't believe me otherwise." He clicked it on while saying, "I'm not against tattoos. When she is old enough, I'll even take her to get her first. I just want her to know that they mean something more than street cred."

Penny started to wonder if this guy even had a daughter, but he'd asked about the right tattoo. Most guys wanted to know about the one on the small of her back or ones in her cleavage. Rarely, did she get to talk about the list on the underside of her forearm. "I got it as a belated thirtieth birthday present." Penny rolled her arm so that he could get a clear shot it. "I wanted to change my life, and these are the three simple rules I used to do it.

GODLESS
BY BRIAN GARRITY

"So I gotta take a leak at the Tizzzle Rizzle, yo? 'Cause of the beer? Get in the can and zip down, pull it out an' just then I notice this guy sittin' on the shitter right there next to me, just sorta looks up an' says 'hey', there's no, like, divider or anything, see? Just me, dick in hand, and the dude next to me, drop-pantsed, shit-farting into a toilet bowl that scares the hell outta me even with my pants on, an' suddenly I gotta piss so bad that I can't fucken' pee. Jesus, I mean, I'm smellin' this guy's shit comin' outta his asshole in real time, an' it's got my cock short-circuited. That shit ever happen to you?"

Barris fingers the trigger-guard, then the trigger of the Kalashnikov in his hands, feeling his appendage come away sticky from the hot metal surface. Probably beer from the party last night, but Christ, when was the last time he checked the action?

Racking the bolt back by hand, he chambers another round as an unspent cartridge spits out the breech and tinkles to the concrete at his feet.

"The fuck, man, ..." Hondo unshoulders the unwieldy RPG he'd been balancing there, and making sure the sinister projectile points skyward, jerks his head at the round still rolling around on the ground, "...you think ammo grows on, ...on, ..." His fingers scratch through thick muttonchops. "...trees?"

"Like you'd know what a tree was." Barris bends and picks the thing up, holding the casing, and raps the bullet-tip, ringed in black to indicate an armor-piercing round, off his front teeth.

"I don't drop a note, and I never waste a round." He slips it into one of the multitude of pockets on his camo's. "Savin' this for something special."

"Trees' one of those fuzzy green things." Hondo grunts, adjusting the heavy backpack, cradling the rocket launcher between his neck and shoulder. He squints against the setting sun down the street at the massive twin overpasses of the Interstate that glitters in a syncopated rhythm from the fractalized reflections of the countless passing windshields.

He checks his watch. "When's this thing gonna go down, anyway?"

Barris presses at something clipped to his ear. "Hey Ray, we got an ETA on the ball here?" He makes a face and rolls his eyes. "Christ Ray, we're sittin' here with our ordnance hanging out for all to see." He sighs, throwing his arm out, notices the Kalashnikov there, and quickly pulls it back in, ducking a little. "Yeah, yeah. We are concealed, but an RPG ain't like stashing a cigarette, you know?"

Eyeing the T-Rock Bar kitty-corner from their position, Hondo swallows dryly watching Barris sign off the ear-thing. "What's she say?"

"She's at Gamma Station with a clear sightline four clicks down the highway. Nothing yet."

"Well fuck ..." Hondo sets the RPG under the smashed wheel-well of the bullet ridden tour bus' hulk they were positioned behind. "... I'm getting a drink."

Barris glares at him. "Yeah, that's a great idea."

"It's just across the street." Hondo's already working his way though the traffic. "It's freakin' hot out here."

"Four minutes! And don't piss off the Goose! He got us that gig next week!" But Hondo's on the other side of the street, out of earshot.

The Triple Rock Social Cub wavers over the broken sidewalk, its battered, peeling exterior striated by countless layers of posters and graffiti tags, testament to generations of displaced souls that had briefly called this club home.

The interior of the bar is cool and dark, with only a few choked rays of sunlight pushing through small, high-set windows on one wall. In contrast, the bottom-lit bottles behind the bar throw up inviting rainbowed hues, and the jukebox crashes out an old 'Naked Raygun' song. A few daytime regulars sit hunched over drinks, the Day-Glo colors of their spiked and mohawked hair interspersed with patches of gray, facial piercings tarnished and drooping, leather jackets cracked and peeling.

Goose is a large barrel-shaped man with thick Buddy Holly glasses and a week or two of scrubby stubble covering his face. He comes out from behind the counter and greets Hondo wearing a 'Free The Memphis Three' T-shirt. Something of a personal affectation, he always wore shirts emblazoned with arcane meanings that nobody but Goose, presumably, understood.

"Hey, Hondo,..." He bellows. "... something cold for you?"

"Yeah, Goose. Chilled Jagermeister."

"Excellent." He bends to work the machine, sets a frosted shot-glass filled with dark liquor on the bar. "Dee-licious!"

"Thanks Goose." He tosses a few bills on the counter, Making sure an ample tip is included.

"Whatcha doin' in the hood, Hondo? Gig isn't till Tuesday."

Hondo checks his watch and throws back the shot. "Big game at the dome today." He coughs, feeling the

Jagermeister hitting home. "We're pre-empting it."

Goose's eyes narrow through the thick glasses. "Awww, you fuckers aren't hitting the overpass again, are you?"

"Goose, it's symbolic. They worship a ball."

"They worship the game."

"Yeah, yeah, yeah. Same difference."

Goose pulls himself up to his full height, dwarfing Hondo, and points to one of the slatted openings in the wall, this one covered by a crudely cut piece of plywood. "Remember your last I-94 excursion?"

"They have that new composite glass, you know, ..."

"You want the drink prices to go up?"

Hondo checks his watch again. "No worries, see? We're hitting it from the other side." He lied. "Gotta go."

"You better be fucken' careful. I mean it Hon." Goose growls.

"Yeah, yeah, yeah. See you Tuesday." He pushes out the door, the heat and light hitting him like a hammer, and he sees Barris waving to him from across the street.

"Two minutes, yo! Flame-on!" He holds the AK-47 at the ready as Hondo preps the RPG.

"So what happened?"

"What?"

"Dude in the can."

"Oh, yeah. Punched him out."

Hondo looks back incredulously as he flips the little sight up. "You punched out some poor guy on the crapper? Kinda harsh, y'think?"

"Well, yeah, had to." Barris gives the banana-clip a tap to make sure it's seated properly. "Was in the middle of our set. Remember when I left the stage between 'Yakuza Girl' and 'War Babies'?"

"Oh. So that's where you went."

"Show must go on."

"True 'an true, 'mon." Hondo levers the RPG back on his shoulder, pointing it through the heat-warped frame of the passenger door's window.

Barris presses the ear-thing. "Ray. Ray, yeah. OK. Yeah, OK, yeah, OK, copy." Eyeing Hondo. "T-minus fifty-five seconds, ...mark."

Thumbing the safety-lever, Hondo takes careful aim at the intersection of the highway bed and its support column. "Thing better work. This package wasn't designed for a structure hit."

"Dante's new recipe. He guarantees results." Barris pulls a pair of high-res Zeiss binoc's out of his back pocket, snaps them open, and, leaning out from behind the wreck's grill, goggles down the highway. "Umm, ... wait for my signal. Lookin' for a break. Much as I want to send these Godfuckers back to their maker, gotta keep the collateral down."

Hondo feels the edge come on, its sharp blade honed slightly by the neutralizing effects of the Jagg. "Window time, Barris."

"Got a break coming. Ready Hon?"

"Righteously, motherfucker." He is breathing calm, his whole being centered around where the sights meet their intended target. Hands rock-steady.

Barris is poised against the grill, still goggling, the rifle coming up in an unconscious gesture.

"On three, ..."

"Wait, ...is that 4/4 or,..."

"Jesus, ...one,"

"Two."

"Three."

Hondo squeezes the trigger and the rocket jumps out of the tube with a shushing sound, its backflash burning an abandoned bus-stop kiosk, and the projectile floats on a fat thread of its own exhaust toward the overpass, where, perhaps, an upward thermal thwarts its course. It glances off the top railing and spirals slowly into an upper-income high-rise project under construction, where the charge detonates with a bright flash about halfway through. The building trembles, and then the southern half of the structure crumbles in slow motion, gray against the sunset.

The delayed thump of the sound-wave hits them.

"Hey man, nice shot."

"No worries,..." Reaching into his backpack, Hondo pulls out the cylinder of the backup rocket, "...it's serendipity. Those Zuppy condo's truly needed some urban renewal, ..."

The bus lurches and the world explodes in a hailstorm of light and sound.

Barris and Hondo reflexively duck, each behind one of the bus' heavy axles as the thing's exoskeleton shreds and actually tears outwards in a rapid series of small sonic booms. A torrent of molten metal sparks crackle through the air around them, hissing into the moist grass, and clanging off a street sign in a tempo that Barris notes, and the frame of the big bus heaves a metallic sigh, its center collapsing to the pavement, sloppily bisected.

The fusillade ceases, and, ears ringing against the abrupt silence, Hondo sees Barris screaming into the ear-thing.

"Cocksucking shitsreaming Jesus, Ray! Yeah, I see 'em!" Body twitching wildly as he tries to peer around the smoldering wreck, Barris is looking a little hysterical and Hondo realizes that he's got his own Sig-Saur 9-mm out, locked and loaded. "Yeah, one, ...no, ...two Centurion patrols directly beneath the overpass, and they got a fucken' Gatling on top a Humvee." He gestures at Hondo. "I dunno. Twenty-millimeter?"

"Nah. Fifty-cal. Twenty would've chewed through the hubs." Hondo chances a glance beneath the undercarriage, pistol in his hand feeling like a pea-shooter, and sure enough, there are two patrol cars lurking behind concrete pylons and the Humvee, standing brazenly in the center of the road, multiple barrels of the Gatling gun a metallic mandala pointed dead-on at them. On the side of the Hummer is painted the logo of the National Church of Athletics, a baroque golden Teutonic cross, orbited by the stylized symbols of a basketball, baseball, football, and a hockey puck.

Then he sees something that immediately freezes his bowels.

"Ah, fuck." He turns to Barris, who is still talking.

"...pinned down. Ray. I can barely move my cock in my pants here, ..."

"Barris, we got a problem."

"What! This isn't enough for you?"

Hondo swallows. "The backup for the RPG?"

"Yeah? Yeah? Yeah?"

"It's out there." He points past the front of the bus.

"Ray, let me get back to you." He squeezes his head around the corner to look where Hondo is pointing and sees the rocket lying about ten yards in front of them in the rubble.

Just how the fuck did that happen?

Barris drops to his stomach, pointing the rifle out of the cleft where the hub meets the ground, to best tactical advantage, and sets the sights on the Hummer's windshield.

"Hon."

"I know."

"You gotta get that, Hon."

"I know."

"INFIDEL SWINE! YOU HAVE ATTEMPTED TO INTERFERE, WITH MALICIOUS BODILY HARM, A SACRED EVENT! SUCH PROFANITY IS AN AFFRONT TO THE LORD, AND SHALL BE DUALLY PUNISHED! ANY SURVIVORS ARE ORDERED TO SURRENDER YOUR ARMS AND STEP AWAY FROM

THE VEHICLE!" The bullhorn squeals as it signs off.

"Fucking hive-mind Centurion drones." Barris switches from full-auto to single shot. The AK-47 bucks hard against his shoulder as he puts one round into the windshield, hearing Hondo take his cue, running behind him. There is a little puff of smoke at the impact point, dead center on the glass, but it barely leaves a scratch. That new composite is some pretty amazing stuff.

With his next two shots, Barris takes out its front tires...

He hears the shrill whine of the Gatling starting up before clearing the shelter of the bus, and Hondo doesn't even get to sprinting speed when the pavement between him and the rocket sort of erupts, big chunks of the stuff leaping into the air of its own accord. Digging in he reverses direction, back to cover, as the maelstrom follows close on his heels...

Armed figures start to emerge from the patrol cars, and Barris is able to put down two with well-placed shots before the others' return fire drives him to shelter. Over the sound of the small caliber rounds stitching through the bus' skin and ringing off the hub, he hears the soft purr of the Gatling as Hondo rushes by almost horizontal to the ground.

This is not good.

Then the cab above him is melting in a shower of

streaking phosphorescence. Back pushed up against the solid steel of the hub, he sees the still-smoldering kiosk in front of him tear itself apart, and for a small eternity Barris is trapped in the womb of a vortex of violence...

Reaching the shelter of the rear axle, Hondo turns and sees Barris disappear in the carnage of the .50 caliber's onslaught. He pulls out the P-226 and moves to the rear bumper, squeezing off three quick rounds, actually hitting one of the patrol Centurions, before ducking back to cover.

Predictably, the .50 caliber starts tearing its way back through the bus towards him and time stretches as he thinks that maybe today wasn't such a great day to get out of bed, not that he really had a bed, it was more of a futon on the floor of their practice space, but still, it was warm and comfortable with a roof overhead, good people to hang with, preferable to dying out here today, and Renee would probably do just fine without him and Barris, after all, he was a drummer, and drummers were always in demand, when all is silent.

A quick glance around confirms that; A] Barris is still alive because, through a parting curtain of debris, he sees him jump up, swinging around the AK-47, and B] The NCA has far too much money and resources to fight intelligently, because in all probability they've just wasted an entire magazine of expensive high-caliber ammo trying to kill two lightly-armed rebels and are currently reloading...

"Barris, the motorcade has stopped a half-click east of your position. You still have a chance of knocking the thing out. Barris? Barris, you still with me?"

Squelching static gives way to a coughing chatter that ends abruptly.

"Ah, yeah Ray, still with you."

"What's your situation? "

"Situation's hot. Ray, but I think we just got a small break."

"Barris, don't be stupid, do it if you can, pull out if you can't."

"Don't think pulling out's really an option here. Ray." More clattering static.

"What's that mean, Barris?"

" Awww, fuck's sake ..."

"Barris? ...Barris, ...Barris!"

Barris is cutting loose with the AK-47 on full auto, peppering the Hummer and drawing fire from the patrols, not really doing much damage but at least preventing them from reloading the Gatling, when a familiar shushing sound causes Hondo to turn and see the rocket propelled grenade floating down the street real low and eerie, haloed by its own booster's corona, coming straight toward them and his mind slips to the warm futon near the back of the space, nestled near the bass cabinet, and then the thing's blurry arc scuds overhead, clearing the ruined frame of the bus by no more than three feet, twisting downward slightly to meet with the hood of the Hummer.

The detonation is impressive and intense, spinning the broken Humvee's body to pancake into the underside of the turnpike in a waft of orange flame, the charred and crumpled remains rebounding to the pavement in a cloud of sound and debris.

"Now dat's da shizzle, MUTHAFUCKA!" Pumping the Kalashnikov, Barris is pointing at him.

Despite his awe at the beauty of the trajectory, Hondo manages to give Barris the finger.

"Well, you sure got it going on in the looks department, but you can't shoot for shit."

Hondo turns at the voice so close it's practically in his ear and he's looking into cool gray eyes sparkling with amusement and mischief.

"Hey, how the fuck ..." And then he recognizes her. Squatting next to him, the battered AR-15 slung over her shoulder, he remembers her on stage in some swank Zuppie backer's private underground club, weathered blonde Rickenbaker bass slung in a similar manner, ripping out some righteous backbeat riffs in her R-girl band. Her shaved and tattooed skull has grown out to a cascade of short, bright red waves, her thick lips have at least a couple more rings through them, and the abbreviated Minnie Pearl dress and Doc Marten combo have given way to a funky species of urban fatigues and combat boots, causing Hondo to speculate on the effectiveness of being camouflaged when walking around with a head of bright neon, but the effect on him is pretty much the same.

Astounding.

"Hey, you play bass in 'TWAT'!'"

"Yeah." She smiles, giving him her hand. "I'm Sliver."

"Hondo, ..." He feels the hard calluses on her slender, delicate fingers. " ...I play bass too."

"Who with?"

"Uh, we really don't have a name yet."

Sliver nods.

"You know, you guys' cover of Fugazi's 'KYEO' is really the shit. I can't believe you do double duty on the vocals." He reflexively runs fingers through his muttonchops. "That's a tough riff."

"Nah. That one's easy."

"You play it in drop D?"

"Huh uh. Drop it down to B."

"Wow."

"Yo, when you guys are done with your date, I could use a little attention here! The Centurions are gonna be pissed!"

Sliver hooks a thumb at Barris. "Who's that?"

"That's Barris." He shrugs. "Singer."

"Oh. Yeah."

"Well he doesn't really sing so much as he grunts and screams, but he's a great guitarist."

"That is important."

Hondo can't believe his luck. Seconds ago he was sure he was ready to suffer a horrible, violent, lonely death, and now here he is, with the woman of his dreams actually saving their lives, a goddess and personal icon of his in the local rock circuit. This is a full-on transcendental moment and Hondo is in love.

"Thanks for saving our asses here. That shot was one in a million."

"Zelda popped that one. My sister." She scrunches up her face. "Singer."

"Yeah? Still,..." He's nodding his head and sitting up, trying to assume a more casual stance, getting a better angle on those cool peepers of hers, and she's rising with him, wry smile on her face, and he's hearing his mouth finish the sentence; "...that was full-on edge." Realizing his terrible mistake but powerless to do anything about it...

The remaining two vehicles sprout three Centurions picking around the Hummer's smoldering remains who at once begin to flank their positions, heavy automatic rifles drawn as Barris glances back at Hondo and that strange commando chick he's yammering with. Incredibly, they both stand up.

Just what the fuck do they think they're doing?

When it happens, Hondo is staring at her breast, or rather her right nipple, which, by the topography it projects through the thin fabric of her designer fatigues, is pierced, when three things occur simultaneously:

He hears from behind him Barris shout something which is cut off immediately by a sharp crack and a large semi-circular swath of Sliver's chest, the epicenter of which is the very nipple that Hondo is staring at, disintegrates in a crimson bouquet with a terrible wet sound. She stands there staring into his eyes, the chasm punched out from her body momentarily defying gravity, and he sees her awareness of impending death pass in her gaze, when the sheen of Sliver's viscera, which has splattered over Hondo's face and chest, starts to run into his eyes. Through the scarlet, viscous haze, she finally surrenders to gravity, body grotesquely collapsing on itself in a chromosomal spiral to the pavement, and the world around Hondo goes gray...

"Barris, talk to me babe."

"Hey, Ray. Yeah, think we're go here in a bit, if Hondo can keep his cock in his pants."

"Not sure I know what you mean by that, boyo, but you better put a rocket in your pocket, 'caus it looks like a couple of Blackbirds are coming in low, hard and fast."

"Shit, you serious? "

"They don't look happy, Barris."

"Duly noted. Ray." Muted crackling and Barris' voice off the set; "Hey, loveb-, .. .ah, God..." More rustling and then static.

"Barris, ...Barris? ...Barris!"

He leans down to her broken body, the only color in the world, the spark, the minute shard of fading iridescence in Sliver's eyes. Her lips tremble with effort and Hondo touches his cheek to hers to hear, transferring a single tear. Skin hot, dry, her last word leaks with the life from her, inflating a bright bubble of blood.

"Squiggle..."

Hondo's mind reels, the bubble pops, her head lolls lifelessly to the side, and the world snaps back into garish color, over-saturated and unreal. The crimson stain smeared around her open mouth an obscene, gore-flecked lipstick...

Barris watches as Hondo stands up from the fallen chick and starts walking nonchalantly, almost casually towards him. Stupid mother fucker, could've been him just as easily as the girl, and here he is, strolling like it's a bright spring day without a care in the world, then he sees that look, the thousand yard stare in his eyes. He knows something's going down.

"Hon, what the fuck you up to?" But he just walks right on past, not hearing, eyes and face blank, slack, he's dragging the rocket launcher behind him, about to step out into the open, practically announcing his presence with the empty metal tube scraping on the ground like that. Then he clears the cover of the bus and there's the flat cracking of the centurions gunfire and the whoop of ricocheting rounds as the ground spits and puffs all around Hondo's feet and Barris just says 'fuck it', checks that he's on full auto, and leaning out, starts unloading his final banana clip ...

Squiggle.

Why the fuck is that word in his head? Hondo's thoughts are a little jumbled. There are noises around him, kind of like the sound of those mutant South American bees they had so many problems with last year, and he keeps getting peppered with gravel and dirt, so there must be a strong wind, but he can't really feel it. He hears the clattering of Barris' Kalashnikov but it's removed, like a memory. Then there's the rocket lying there, right in front of him. All kinds of stupid, leaving it there like that, and as he's bending to pick it up he discovers the RPG in his hand and it comes in a flash, why he's here, why the rocket's lying in front of him, when something tags him in the left calf hard enough to spin him completely upside down, planting his face in the gravel...

Mentally counting down, just an approximation really, 'caus the AK-47 fires too rapidly to actually count, and it is the heat of the battle, Barris is trying to pace himself, keeping his concentration down the sights of the barrel, not looking, not thinking of how Hondo's probably being chewed to pieces by the volley of gunfire he's trying to suppress.

Two patrol cars. Three centurions. And half, correction, less than half a clip left.

And, of course, one psycho stupid motherfucking bass player lurching around the field of fire like Superman with a hangover.

The unexpected upside to this is that with Hondo acting as bait, the centurions are going all out wild, giving up their positions, and in quick succession Barris manages to put a round through the helmet of guy #1 from car A, giving credence to an earlier argument with Hondo as to the reasoning behind Barris' preference for armor-piercing ammunition, then he actually hits the rifle of guy #3 from car B, shattering the cheap Government-issue carbine to splinters, rendering him temporarily useless.

The last guy is good. He's got technique and Barris wasting ammo as he ducks and slips shots through his suppression when finally, he makes a fatal mistake, and, dead-on in his sights, Barris squeezes the trigger.

The dry click of the hammer against the empty chamber carries like a sonic boom across the void. Last Guy's head snaps up in sync with his rifle, and Barris is looking down the dark maw of certain death. Though the moment seems to stretch around a mobius-strip of eternity, he barely has time to breathe or even blink before Last Guy's own impotent clack answers him from across the far side of the battlefield.

Another thing those cheap Government-issue carbines do well is jam.

For a wild moment each considers the other incredulously, then Last Guy is frantically clawing at his ordnance and Barris is rifling through the countless chambers of his camo's for the single round he'd pocketed what seems like centuries ago, but in fact was only a few minutes earlier. Front to back, top to bottom he finds his wallet, keys, lighter, a drink ticket dated yesterday wrapped around a severely weathered condom wrapper, small notebook with ballpoint pen stuck in the spiral, sunglasses, cell phone, pot stash, half pack of cigarettes, a small cache of picks, and, ...spare change?

OK. Why does he have so many damn pockets, and how could he commit such a serious breach of combat etiquette as bringing loose change on a mission?

A quick check in on Last Guy and Barris' heart goes black. From the smug expression on his face, the way he snaps the clip home, guesses that the carbine's short-comings have been trouble-shot, that he's just run out of time. Then his fingers find the elusive brass cylinder wedged in the little pocket intended for lighters that no one ever uses and again he's looking down the bore of Last Guy's gun when a howling ululation breaks the silence and Barris has time to chamber the round and consider the possibility that Hondo is still alive when the barrel wavers slightly in the direction of the sound.

No time for precision here, so he just goes for the body shot, putting it through Last Guy's bullet-proof vest, seeing his surprise and shock as the carbine ejaculates in his hand, stitching a line of fire across the pavement and up the side of the bar, popping out one of the three remaining windows.

Shit. The Goose is gonna be pissed....

Hondo is beyond pain and way past pissed.

He keeps seeing Sliver and the way her chest exploded, the terror passing in her eyes, and the cocoon of calm around him shatters.

By some freakish trick of the light, bullets are visible scything the air around him in clustered little time-signatures, the faint snapping of their origins syncopating with the noise of Barris' Kalashnikov.

He is screaming as he pushes himself up, a throat tearing, lung searing roar of pure animal rage, expelling gravel and a muddy mucal flow from his mouth, feeling the hot flow of blood down his leg. Lurching forward, fingers grappling on the ground for the rocket, raising the length of the RPG, sliding it home in the tube against his shoulder, sights up and calibrated, distant awareness of an aural vacuum, lack of sound, bodies on the ground, feeling fusion, connection with the target, knowing with certainty even before the trigger is pulled that the trajectory is true.

The overpass blossoms petals of pulverized pewter heaving the heavy concrete deck-plates upward through whirling clouds of shattered I-beam fragments, the blast pushing him back to the ground with a hot hand, the sound larger even than the last Husker Du concert he'd seen as a kid, decking finally dominoing itself into the valley of the underpass in huge, slow-motion monoliths, pushing out a mushrooming earthbound cumulonimbus cloud of debris, obscuring the carnage and settling over them.

A real-life, real-time fade-out...

"You did it. Jesus-fuck. You fucken' did it."
Goose's ghostly form emerges from the drifting

nimbus of flotsam, the bar a dull backlit geometric shape behind him.

Hondo's carrying the remains of Sliver, leaking whatever fluids hadn't already soaked into the ground, reeking because the body had voided itself in death, Barris plodding mechanically next to him shucking empty clips into his pockets, slap of the Blackbirds blades through the air, approaching blindly somewhere through the murk.

"Roll it motherfuckers! In the bar!" Goose's mass is moving with surprising speed towards them, collecting and displacing swirling eddies of ash and soot, hands on the ends of outstretched arms gesturing them to him, and Barris notices the darker streaks leaking out from under his glasses over the gray of his cheeks.

"Hey Goose, .. .you,.. .uh, crying?"

"Nevermind, nevermind,.. .those Blackbirds, .. ."He thuds to a halt when he sees the mess in Hondo's arms. " ...'th fuck?"

Barris shrugs and Hondo just regards him with glazed eyes.

Huge ham hands slap at his face and for a moment it seems like Goose is doing a little bow in front of them, fingers squashing his eyes, jiggling the glasses up on his forehead, voice muffled beneath thick palms.

"Jeez fuck, ..." Then with that amazing ability reserved for gigantic bartenders he is behind them, collaring each in a bouncers cuckold, propelling them both towards the doorway, now surrounded by a shadowy phalanx of regulars. " .. .hearin' that Gatlin', I think,... no I know you guys are dead. Then when you drop that overpass I think I'm fucken' dead, then I see you alive but, .. .but with that poor, .. .Christ, you two got me on a fuck of a roller-coaster ri-"

A sound cuts the air around them, a voice slicing time, a polytonal contralto that to Hondo's practiced ear is pure beauty as it steps across angelic scales in a winding bel canto, disintegrating with a spiraling arpeggio, especially considering it is a scream of guttural terror and grief.

Standing before them, ice-blue eyes wide on what's left of Sliver, is the only pure-blooded Caucasian Hondo's ever seen, the RPG tube in her doll-like fingers a startling contrast to the delicate folds of the antique Versace she is wearing, cascading platinum hair and flawless ivory skin casting a luminous halo in the falling ash.

This is Zelda, Sliver's sister...

"Nice job, boy-yo's. Better late that never. The game is FUBAR with all that traffic back-up, and no apparent collateral. You-know-who is gonna be pumped. Hey, you getting this? "

Squelch.

"Barris? ...Barris, ...Barris!"

Squelch.

"Over-and-fuck-you-out!"

Ill Communication
By Bob Lipski

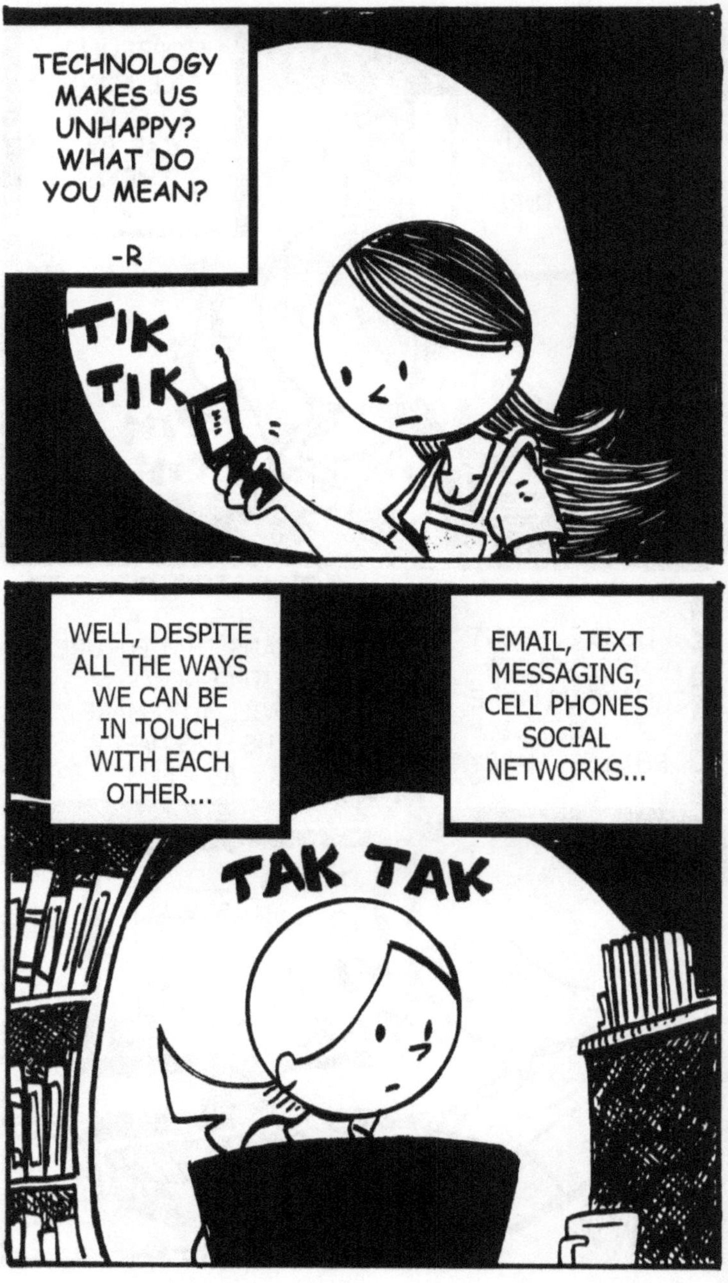

THINKER'S LURE
BY TOIANNA GUMP

*Dedicated to my Dad,
who taught me to seek my own Truth,
rather than to accept Truth as defined by others
and especially as handed down by authority figures.*

1.

For better or for worse, he was home. As he breathed in the familiar aroma of walleye and fries across the street, pierogis and red cabbage on the other corner of Western and Selby, Guy fixed his gaze on Nina's Cafe and Coffee, which now bore the gleaming, metallic, fish-shaped sign "Thinker's Lure."

Hokey and ironic, Guy thought to himself about the change of business names, then thoughtfully and barely audibly, added "creepy" aloud.

Although his son Nate had led him to believe that he was safe to return for a brief visit to St Paul and secondly that Thinker's Lure retained much of Nina's original flavor for provocative debate, Guy felt gut level apprehension, like his visit was a terrible mistake.

From the time he had boarded the Greyhound in Berkeley to the time he stepped onto University Ave, both his stomach and jaw had clenched, despite painstaking lengths he had taken to alter his appearance and despite the decoy person left in his place, with a voice box likeness to do his job so that those scrutinizing his every move would believe he was still in his Berkeley office.

He had begun playing cat and mouse regularly and seemingly effectively with those circulating the Regulations of Uniformity ever since his sudden move to California without his family.

Admittedly dumb, he had not established a good cover story and consequently, had not gone discreetly.

He knew that his move to California had been a clear sign to the Committee that he was indeed a renegade.

Days before he left, he had received a sign of his own. He had been hot and entering rush hour traffic on I94 west to St Paul was a nightmare. And as he pulled up to the University Club for a quick drink with the guys and pulled into a place on Summit hill, his mini van sputtered and threatened not to brake. It felt like that moment in a roller coaster when the car is teetering right before racing down a steep part. In that moment, Guy had a kind of vision, in which he saw himself losing control of his vehicle, the car flying boundary less down the hill into traffic, and crashing into a semi. The mini van was crushed like a soda pop can and he...had forced his mind to change course before he could see the details of what happened to him. Without thinking, he had pulled out of the parking place on a precipice, where his vehicle was rebelling against having been stopped. And he drove home to pack.

He had known the price tag attached for his decision to walk away from his life as one of the suits at 3M and spending his spare time hobnobbing at the art deco bar of the Commodore Club in Banana Republic khakis, Ralph Lauren polo shirts, and sporty oxfords.

But he also realized that he would face a like fate, or worse, if he stayed in St Paul because when cornered and forced to choose between retaining individuality and the ability to think for himself or support the Regulations of Uniformity, he would go down fighting for his right to spend the remainder of his life as himself, not some politically correct clone. Three days later, he was on a bus headed to California.

2.

Now as he stood outside the door of Thinker's Lure completely unrecognizable as the same man who had fled with the intention of never returning, he felt somehow transparent.

He had put this plan into operation successfully so many times that he had lost count, but never to destinations that rendered him vulnerable or sentimental.

He flashed on thinkers he had known, who had disappeared somewhere into the woodwork before he left town and once church and politics had merged completely together to form the Committee of Twelve and the Regulations of Uniformity.

Anything could have become of them. People who were a threat to those in power disappeared all the time. And the Committee was composed of the wealthiest, most powerful and influential individuals in the Twin Cities, those who had decided for decades which issues were most important and the viewpoint everyone would share in practice.

The Committee's self appointed mission was to transform the community into one united mindset, by forcing everyone through insidious means to adhere to the Regulations of Uniformity they had created and appeared intent on establishing statewide for what they deemed the greater good.

Popularity of the Regulations of Uniformity was growing rapidly and spreading, like disease, in Guy's mind.

The media raved about the merge being an answer to prayer and they pointed their cameras to freshly painted apartment complexes with colorful playgrounds from Frogtown to Robbinsdale, grants for integrated schools, and food for seniors.

But Guy recognized the situation for what it was. Regardless of how many puppies and little kids Committee representatives held, Guy knew that those behind the scenes pulling the strings were just negotiating another business deal, in which a few key players were becoming much wealthier.

Guy's apprehension was that the worst part was yet to come. He had sensed from the start that this went further than corporate takeover.

The self-elected Committee of power mongers had set up shop, in his mind, to create what in their eyes was the perfect society, whereby everything was done for the majority by a select few. Especially the thinking.

He sighed and forced himself to set aside all of the terrifying possibilities becoming reality. In this moment, he did not want to focus on thinkers, renegades, or the forces silencing anyone who opposed them. He wanted to just collect his thoughts before returning to the business at hand, more heart wrenching than all of the Committee issues that had put his life at risk.

He had returned to St Paul as a gesture to show his son Nate that, despite appearances, he did care about his wife and son. Although his son did not overtly say it, Guy knew Nate blamed him for his mother's death. He felt it in his gut when Nate first spoke during their last phone conversation to firm up plans about Guy's visit. He could tell he would not get another chance to rebuild a relationship with Nate.

And if he lost Nate, what was the point? He was fighting not only for his freedoms, but even more, for the generations to come, especially his own son.

3.

Despite Nate's coldness, Guy had wanted to reach through the telephone wires and hold his boy in his arms. It was almost impossible for him to wrap his mind around Nate having become a man since he had been gone.

Guy cleared his throat and flashed on the irony of how Nate had described Thinker's Lure.

Nate had said that the joint retained the same appeal for the same kinds of rabble rousers, as though they were a group of misfit losers, who had nothing better to do.

In reality, Nina's was filled at any given time with individualists, who were unalike in most every other way except for their enjoyment of debate and defending their positions. They thrived on opposing points of view.

So, how could his son see them as all the same? Not to mention as his implication that they were the so called bad guys.

He sighed. This was the price for having left his son in this God forsaken community.

It was the Committee that was bringing about lack of variety, predictability, and monotony, in order to make their job of manipulating everyone easier. A community full of stray individualists, asking too many questions and challenging their authority, posed problems and meant roadblocks or revolt.

Nate's take on Nina's aside, Guy was surprised

almost to the point of suspicion that Thinker's Lure still retained its draw for renegades and thinkers. He couldn't suppress all of his suspicion about why strangers Guy had met, while hitchhiking from Northern California to Minnesota and residents of Paradise Peak, formerly Summit Hill, spoke fairly openly about Thinker's Lure continuing to be a haven for independent thinkers. What was wrong with this picture?

Was it possible that there was still a modicum of freedom and right to individuality? Guy could not get the nagging question out of his mind about why the Committee of Twelve would not have cleaned up and cleared out all places like Thinker's Lure, which they clearly designated as renegade and therefore a threat to their cause.

The Committee knew better than anyone that Nina's Cafe & Coffee had always attracted an eclectic assortment of writers, artists, college professors, hobos, eccentrics, and crazies since the recalcitrant madame had set up shop at Nina's originally.

At any given time between 6am and 10 pm, a person could wander comfortably into conversations amongst writers, college professors, artists, and scientists, who debated religion and politics, ways to improve and save the world, discussed how TV and technology in general were crippling the young, how resourcefulness, creativity, self reliance, and thinking were becoming obsolete. Nina's had always been dependable for individuals to find the thinkers - also known as radicals.

Funny how true the saying had turned out to be that those who were wealthy were considered to be eccentric, and those who were poor were labeled crazy. Nowadays, defining labels and the consequences were even more straightforward. There was uniform, and there was renegade. So why would thinkers be able to meet so openly and publicly?

Thinkers were probably the singularly greatest threat to the Committee of Twelve, given their absolute and passionate opposition. He felt safe enough. The only one who would know his identity was Nate.

4.

Guy smiled to himself, as he remembered the exact moment at home in the Dinkytown district that his mother had looked up from her game of solitaire at the kitchen table and told Guy that Minnesotans weren't supposed to move, unless it was just to another part of the state. His mother had warned him his move to California was not a good idea.

He had found her sentiments charming and naïve, and like she was still seeing him at fifteen.

She was, of course, opposed to him leaving his family, but seemed to understand once he explained his desire to help in the opposition of the committee of Twelve. She and Guy's Dad had voiced concern quietly for the future of their grandchildren.

Too bad she had not lived long enough to see Guy return. Now in this moment that he was on Minnesota soil again, he understood on a deeper level what she had meant. But he was not sorry that he had gone. It had still been the right decision, the only ethical decision, if he really cared about Nate.

Otherwise, he had ensured before he made the trip to St Paul that he looked like someone altogether different. University of Minnesota students his mother had sent his way had reworked his identity in paperwork. In fact, he had become someone other than the man who left St Paul fifteen years earlier.

That led Guy back to fleetingly vague details he knew so far about the explosion and huge ensuing fire that had occurred at Nina's one Saturday night. As of yet, all the investigators would say an in depth investigation was underway.

One hundred individuals had died in the explosion, and former owner June had disappeared, according to a few newcomers who had recently joined the thinker's underground group in California.

The last Guy had heard, no one knew for sure whether or not June's body was one of the one hundred found, and people were not asking questions.

All that was known for sure was that the shop had closed. Temporary shades were set up to cover all of the windows until one week later when Thinker's Lure opened.

As a local fireman, Nate would know more and probably be able to answer some of his questions.

Something about the look of Thinker's Lure made Guy pause momentarily in the doorway, before he strode inside and inhaled both the aroma of gourmet coffee and seemingly familiar ambiance. In fact, he felt strange, like he was forcing himself to walk against a strong current to get inside.

The somehow bone chilling difference was empty space. No more mounds of clutter, that once included art exhibits and posters on the walls, fliers for rallies and demonstrations, wall to wall bookshelves, filled to capacity with centuries of mind blowing revelations and a gold mine of human dilemma, laid out in treasure maps of problems articulated and alluding to brilliant solutions. Guy liked Scandinavian sparse. But the emptiness here, coupled with silence, somehow made him think of death.

Most disturbing was the lack of sound, as though everyone was holding his breath. Guy associated laughter and playful bantering, pounding on laptop keys, and music with Nina's. He recalled noise filling every crevice of space. There had been always been loud discussions, debates, newspapers crinkling, writers rifling through drafts of their manuscripts, and bookworms turning the page, like their lives depended upon what they read next.

"So, this is what comes of silence and empty space," he mumbled under his breath as he looked at the space, empty except for a pole of electrical outlets alongside the brick wall that now served as a room divider and obviously replaced the stone fireplace in the center of the main room. Electricity, gloom, and thoughts of mortality.

5.

Quiet before a storm flashed through his mind. Did the quiet signify anything ominous? Or was it just lack of sound? Clearly he was plenty paranoid, but was their cause? During their brief and uncomfortable conversation for the first time in several years, his son Nate had assured him that he was safe to return for Alice's funeral.

Guy had thought about not coming until he visualized the adult version of Nate's little five year old face he had walked away from fifteen years earlier. He could picture all too easily both the abandonment and subsequent resentment that Nate must feel and could not bear heaping on another dollop that might mean the difference between him ever having any chance to become close to Nate again.

As though cued, a white haired elderly man, who looked about 90 and resembled a well-groomed Einstein with glasses, fired at a young man, "To hell with the internet! It's distracting. It's meaningless. It's not real. It's in the air somewhere." Then grumbling, he returned to reading his book and turned the pages with deliberation, as though to punctuate his former remarks, daring anyone looking to stop him.

Guy saw himself in about forty years. He understood the old man's voracious appetite for reading, which in Guy's case, extended to strong convictions that led ultimately to the day he decided he could no longer costume himself in the suits and tennis wear, or play his part in the elitist group at the University Club on top of Summit Hill, where the cream was getting separated from the milk and deals were happening to rid the Twin Cities of rebels in order to smooth the path for the Committee of Twelve to become statewide consultants or seize control, as Guy saw it. Between the vision of crashing his mini van and getting obliterated and the rubbish he was hearing, Guy had not even stuck around to hear the details.

He had returned to his family's small apartment that looked drained of all color and had tried reasoning with Alice once again about leaving the Ladies of Ordinance, and Father Beatty, to join him on his quest to California, where an expansive underground society was building steam and preparing a national revolution against the Order of Uniformity.

Father Beatty or Captain Beatty, as he was nicknamed for his years in the army and even more for his domineering personality, had promised Alice a huge, low-cost home in the Arms of Sanctuary complex, directly across the street from the catholic school Nate had just started attending.

Guy could not help but muse about the irony again, as he struggled to keep images of Alice in the burning apartment out of his mind. He had always heard that most fire victims were unconscious from the smoke fumes long before the actual fire reached them. He hoped Alice had not suffered. Fortunately Nate had missed that call for whatever reason.

Guy stepped in line behind two elderly ladies discussing baseball from fifty years ago. One of them said she had waited after every game for players to come out, and she had talked to everyone on the Twins team so many times that Joe Mauer had broken down and come over for dinner a few times. She went on to remark about what a pity it was that the New York Yankees had bought their wins and had been responsible, in her mind at least, for the national loss of interest in baseball. Her friend had responded, "yeah, but what about those Twins? What a team."

While thumbing through the Committee of Twelve or COT news, which was presented as objective news coverage and in truth amounted clearly to propaganda to support their cause, Guy reflected on how Alice had been tidying a few things compulsively when he walked into their apartment. She had not even looked up when he had said, "My ride leaves in an hour. So, I guess I should get going. I'll call you in a few days with how to reach me, in case..." He had paused and closed his eyes. He didn't want to leave them here or anywhere within a thousand miles of Father Beatty. He choked back tears and added, "I'll call you."

6.

He started out, then stopped in the doorway, turned around, and once again pleaded, "Alice, come with me. Just walk away from all of this. Come to California. You and Nate and I will be okay as long as we have one another."

Alice had lifted her head, but said nothing. She looked out the window at nothing in particular.

As Guy hurried down the stairs of their front porch and onto the sidewalk, Nate came running from the backyard, then froze in place with a blank expression, which was difficult for Guy to read.

Guy hugged Nate's stiff body, kissed his forehead, and reassured him that they would see one another again soon, although he did not believe it.

Wow. He had underestimated how choked up he would become and how quickly. By the time he got his bearings, it would probably be time to leave. The intensity of how torn he had been all these years about having gone to California struck him hard now that he was back. He knew that leaving would be much more difficult than having come. He would leave as soon as possible to finish what he had started: defending freedom to be individuals, make choices, and think independent of the Committee of Twelve.

When his turn came, Guy purchased an iced mocha from a friendly college-age girl and found the smallest table for two he could so he could be assured of no company. As he sipped his coffee, he looked out the large picture window. As he had years earlier, Guy thought about how Thinker's Lure was located strangely close to the St. Paul Cathedral, an edifice that had always served a counter purpose to Nina's in his mind.

While Nina's had been a platform for thinkers, the Cathedral had been the gathering place for those willing to allow others to think for them and to inform them about what they believed voting constituents needed to know to make the right choices.

Now the Cathedral stood vacant and dark, looming over the city, as a frightening reminder of how everything had fallen apart.

While living in St Paul, Guy had mused oftentimes about the proximity of the Cathedral to the state capitol building, like lovers magnetized to each other and meeting secretly in the middle of the night. Likeness between the two buildings and Rosary rappers walking in procession between the two fortresses had created an energy between the two seats of power hungry authority figures.

Guy finished his coffee in one gulp and studied the clientele as inconspicuously as he could.

Where was Nate? Guy had known before he arrived

that Nate would not be awaiting him with open arms, but somehow he had assumed Nate would be first to arrive. Maybe the fire station had a call. But wouldn't he have called Guy or even called this shop?

Fragments of one conversation in particular caught his attention. He could have sworn he heard two young guys talking about how one of the Twins players had come over for dinner at their house back in the day and 'how about those Twins'. Had one of the Twins died recently? Were any of them from that period still playing and why the sudden focus on them?

He closed his eyes for a moment and heard parts of several nearby conversations. One about deluxe memory enhancement logs that increased the recipient's self confidence and positive outlook. A slender college student in a sleeveless black leather jacket and rings in his nose and eyebrows was talking in familiar code about an underground group Guy knew was opposed to the COT and the Code of Uniformity.

7.

Guy wondered where the Committee of Twelve was meeting these days to review community regulations and to discuss any renegade activity or deviation from the Code of Uniformity.

Then the dam broke down in his mind and he could not help the flood of thoughts and emotions that took over. What could they have done differently to have prevented things from getting this far out of hand?

When money had been tight and all of the churches, except for the Catholic church, had collapsed the Catholic churches had grown worried about their hold on the community, as their schools were forced to close as relative independents. They were forced to pool their resources and condense into one big community.

However, as the church's ability to maintain stability was still threatened, what could they have done differently, besides listening to politicians? There must have been something, given all of the plans and promises to subsidize them and allow them to retain their power, in exchange for the church giving them the credibility they needed.

Even then, the question talked about quietly behind closed doors remained. Had the church understood the terms?

That damned Catholic convert's group that met at the University Club on Summit, the P.G. Wodehouse Society headed by the lunatic referred to as Jeeves, was where the Committee had begun forming and probably somewhere amidst all of the back-scratching politics at the unofficial continuation of the meeting, further down Selby at the Happy Gnome.

The P.G. Wodehouse Society was where Twin Cities attorneys, doctors, priests, deacons, and University of St. Thomas students gathered, supposedly for fun to discuss the writings of P.G. Wodehouse, then continued late into the night over drinks and debate at the Gnome.

However, Guy and many others had heard the rumors and always known about the group's real elitist agenda. Mostly men in positions of power locally attended and somewhere during the course of hobnobbing, senators and archbishops had begun discussions about ways to obliterate not only dangerous, gang traffic areas like Frogtown and Little Somalia, but also how to take down the college and University districts.

Rumors had circulated in underground groups that they had discussed how to utilize memory stations to discourage anything they considered to be radical thinking or in other words, any thinking that differed from their own. Many thought the group was messing somehow with cerebral parts of the brain and removing parts of the frontal lobe.

The society's thinking seemed to be that the community could run like a well-oiled machine, if there was uniformity of actions, which came most easily when everyone thought alike and shared common goals for the good of the community. They believed individualists served only to disrupt and pollute civilized society.

The Bishop had sanctioned funding to help families in Frogtown's St. Dismas school and church community to form a commune that circled and insulated the old, conservative parish, rectory and convent. All of the homes and land three blocks out in every direction from St. Dismas had been purchased in the past couple of years for this purpose.

At first, Hmong and Black gangs had fought the intrusion and takeover of their territory in every way they knew from breaking windows and spray painting graffiti all over the church's outer concrete walls, to intimidating residents with machine guns and terrorizing families.

8.

Suddenly the fighting stopped, and no one heard anything more from any of the gangs. Even most gang members seemed too afraid to find out what had happened to those who had disappeared, let alone take revenge.

Many believed that when the society morphed into the Committee of Twelve, one of the actions the Committee took was to set an example to locals about the consequences they faced if they went up against the Code of Uniformity or interfered with what they spoke of as their "divine purpose."

When two stragglers from the street who looked like they had not bathed in a decade walked by and were talking about one of the Twins players having come over for dinner and how the Yankees had contributed to the end of baseball, Guy knew it was time to leave. Something was terribly wrong with this picture. Nate was not coming.

Then the well groomed Einstein rose suddenly from his seat, obviously agitated, looking towards the door, and cried, "Look at yourself in the mirror, why don't you, to see what's missing?!" Then he began ranting and raving passages from the Bible that Guy thought might be from the book of Revelation.

Simultaneously, Guy watched everyone in the room scurrying towards the two exits, as he turned his gaze to the door and saw a young man standing in the doorway in full fireman gear, except for his gloves, helmet and face mask he held in his hand.

Casually Nate combed through his hair with his empty hand, while coldly and sarcastically remarking, "Father, I look good as a fireman, don't you think?"

Unable to move, Guy watched as Nate signaled to ten men behind him to pass. Also dressed in fireman attire, each walked purposefully to a different part of the room and dumped gallon jugs of gasoline.

"Sorry, I am late, father. I was preparing because there is going to be a fire."

As he dumped a gallon of gasoline around the pole, he said "bet you miss the fireplace that used to be here."

He laughed maniacally as he pulled the grilling lighter out of his pocket.

"Time for a real facelift for this place."

The End

Other titles by Onyx Neon Press

Gigapolis
by S. Christopher

Gravitas
by S. Christopher

ONYX
NEON

For more information on
the authors or to keep up with
Onyx Neon Press visit
www.onyxneon.com

www.ingramcontent.com/pod-product-compliance
Lightning Source LLC
Chambersburg PA
CBHW051847170626
46807CB00003B/1395

* 9 7 8 0 9 7 7 9 2 0 1 4 3 *